Ninja at First Sight

An Origin Story
Knitting in the City #4.75

By PENNY REID

Caped Publishing

Made in the United States of America

Print Edition: January 2016
Print ISBN: 978-1-942874-14-0

~Dedication~

To Mr. Reid.

Prologue – August 1997

"I DON'T LIKE this. I feel like I've been lied to." My mother said this loudly, glaring at the open door to the suite area. I was certain her voice carried down the hall. "I've never heard of *co-ed dorms*. It's disgusting. They might as well just hand out condoms and host an orgy."

I was silent, though I was tempted to point out that my university did hand out condoms during orientation. Really, the goal was to encourage her to leave as soon as possible. Any mention of condoms, regardless of how much passive-aggressive joy it might bring me, would be counterproductive.

"I see your face. Just you wait." She glared, pointing her finger at me.

I lifted my eyebrows and shrugged. "What?"

"Just you wait until you have children, then you'll understand. When you have your own children, you'll be calling me up and apologizing for everything you've put me through."

Turning back to the box of books I was unpacking, I muttered under my breath, "Yeah, that's not likely."

I heard footsteps approach and turned toward the open door just in time to see my father enter, throwing his thumb over his shoulder. "There sure are a lot of young men hanging around here. When I went to Cornell, boys weren't allowed to just wander around in the women's dorm. They weren't allowed in at all."

My father winked, obviously knowing this statement would drive my mother crazy. He lived for pushing her buttons. I gave him a pained smile.

"They're not hanging around, George." She leaned closer to him and loud-whispered, "They live here!"

"Live here? Huh…" His eyes widened with what I knew was mock surprise, and he added thoughtfully, "I need to go back to college."

"George!" She smacked him on the shoulder, her forehead a maze of consternation wrinkles. "How can you joke about this? Fiona could be raped, murdered, or worse!"

I frowned at my mother, tempted to ask what she had in mind that was worse than rape or murder. She was a reactionary, always had been. She followed the mantra of react first, think later (if at all). I loved her, but she was exhausting.

"Okay." I said loudly, "Time for you to leave. Let me walk you to the elevator."

My mother huffed, and I could see the anxiety on her face. My heart softened a little—a very, very little—at her expression, but hardened when she said, "Fiona, you don't know how much time you have left on this earth. What if the tumor comes back? What are you going to do? Hmm? You'll be helpless, alone, with strangers. This is your last chance to come home with us. If you insist on staying here, we will follow through with our decision to cut you off. I mean it; you'll have no support from us, and you'll have no insurance."

I held my tongue and peeked over her shoulder to my dad. He gave me the faintest of head shakes, his eyes narrowing just a smidge. Although he didn't agree with my decision to go to college so far from home, he'd pulled me aside last week and assured me that he wouldn't be removing me from his work insurance policy.

He'd even offered to provide financial assistance as well, but I turned him down. I didn't want to cause any more drama in their relationship. My academic scholarship would cover the bulk of my expenses. Plus I had my sponsorship dollars from when I was still an athlete, the accounts just recently signed over to me on my eighteenth birthday.

Like my mother, my father was overprotective. Unlike my mother, his decisions were typically grounded in well-reasoned arguments, facts, and reality. But his overprotectiveness of me was largely due to guilt, guilt that he'd been mostly absent for my childhood.

I'd observed that much of what parents do, their decisions and actions, is driven by guilt—either directly because of it or as a means to escape it.

My eyes returned to my mother and I cleared my face of expression. "I know, mother. We've already discussed your feelings on the matter." She'd told me how angry she was with me every day since I told them of my decision to move seven states away from home, where no one knew me, and I could be just another college freshman. "I know how you feel. Now it's time for you to go."

"You're breaking my heart!" My mother said dramatically.

I tried to keep my voice as gentle as possible as I ushered—pushed—them out of my room, out of the suite, down the hall, and to the elevator. "You'll be fine. I'll call you."

"I won't take your calls. I don't want to hear from you if you won't listen to reason. And don't try calling your sister. I don't want you polluting her mind."

A pang of homesickness and longing—for my sister—hit me square in the chest, and my voice wasn't exactly steady as I responded, "Okay, I won't call."

"You'll die here, Fiona. At a *state* school!" my mother sobbed. I tried not to roll my eyes.

I didn't know which she felt was worse: the fact that my

brain tumor might reoccur or that I was going to a state university (in Iowa) rather than to Vassar.

My dad pressed the button for the lobby and wrapped his arm around my mother's shoulders, addressing me, "You should call; don't listen to her. She's just upset."

"Don't patronize me, George!" She snapped, pulling away from him.

The doors slid shut while they continued to argue, and I closed my eyes, my forehead hitting the hallway wall. I could hear their bickering for the first few seconds as the elevator descended.

I sighed, and it felt like the first real breath I'd ever taken.

Part 1: Two ninjas walk into a bar...

PEOPLE COMPLETELY FASCINATE me.

Take my college roommate, Dara, and her boyfriend, Hivan. They had sex in our dorm room all the time. It didn't matter if I was asleep, and it didn't matter if I was at my desk studying. Usually Dara was topless by the time they made it in the room. At first, Dara would be surprised by my presence and try to gently ask me to leave. Meanwhile, Hivan asked me if I'd like to join them.

I declined.

But it wasn't the nonstop sex that fascinated me. In fact, as an eighteen year old who'd never been kissed or had a boyfriend, I was a smidge envious of the sex part.

They fascinated me because 1) they saw nothing odd or inappropriate about interrupting my sleep, studying, or privacy at all hours of the day or night, and 2) Hivan cheated on Dara all the time.

By the third week their relationship followed a predictable cycle. For three days everything would be fine. On the fourth or fifth day, Dara would burst into the room crying and sobbing and screaming, throwing anything within reach. She'd tell me that she was through with Hivan because he'd cheated on her.

He would eventually show up at some point during the next two days. I would leave. They'd have sex. Everything would be fine for the next few days, and the cycle would repeat.

Also fascinating, by the end of the first month, all pretext evaporated. They'd just plow into the room and go at it as soon as they'd breached the threshold, regardless of whether I was present. Sometimes, if I was already asleep, I'd put on my headphones, blast music, and cover my face.

The part of me that had a voracious appetite for observing and studying people was enthralled by their theatrics. It almost seemed like Hivan created the drama and excitement because he sensed Dara thrived on it. I didn't understand this, why someone would crave this kind of drama, and so I studied them.

Honestly, the situation didn't bother me once I adjusted to it as my reality. In addition to my fascination, I figured it was all part of the genuine college experience. I supposed I was odd in this way. Situations that typically made other people uncomfortable or angry or offended were of intense interest to me.

I'd always been an observer of human nature, more content to sit back and watch than get involved, but I suspected my upbringing was the root cause. I never had many friends because I'd had very few opportunities to make friends. Social interaction, social order, and social norms and dynamics were a mystery to me.

Usually, I would discuss my observations with Hannah, my sister. But every time I called my mother would pick up the line and listen in.. Therefore, we hadn't talked at all for the last four months about anything of significance and I missed her perspective.

I understood athletes. I understood drive and competition and ambition to succeed and to have a singular purpose. But I didn't understand this world of normal and varied interests because I'd never lived in it.

The other two girls in my suite were Beth, a perpetually anxious and serious-minded pre-med freshman, and Fern.

Fern was Beth's opposite in every way.

Where Beth was reed thin and dressed conservatively, Fern was voluptuous and dressed like a 1950's pinup. Where Beth was studying all the time and waking up early to exercise, Fern hardly ever went to class and frequently staggered into the suite intoxicated at all hours of the day and night.

I think Beth and Fern got on each other's nerves; Beth left by week six, opting to move into a single room elsewhere on campus as soon as it became available.

Fern told me in passing that she was only going to college because her parents insisted that she at least try it for one or two years. What she really wanted to do was become a Scientologist minister, and she didn't need a college degree for that. As such, Fern decided to major in Latin. She thought this was hilarious.

Mostly, I kept to myself; watching, considering, unobtrusively attempting to solve the mysteries of those around me, and trying to soak up every day.

Being alone in a sea of strangers didn't trouble me. I didn't crave social interaction, but I truly enjoyed watching people. I was enormously grateful for the freedom of finally living away from home, for being around people who didn't know me and therefore didn't look at me like I was breakable or about to explode or didn't understand that brain tumors aren't contagious.

Here I was, just another college freshman, and all the normal nuttiness and theatrics and drama felt like a gift.

***

"WHAT ARE YOU doing?"

I blinked at the voice and found Fern staring down at me, her bright red-painted lips curved in an impressively large smile.

I shifted in my seat; my eyes flickered to the wall clock above my desk space. I was sitting in the general suite area, curled up on my desk chair while Hivan and Dara screamed at each other. If it hadn't been January and the weather hadn't been sub-zero, I would have hiked to the library. My other option was the study rooms downstairs in the lobby of the dorm; however, on a day like this, those rooms were usually booked for hours.

"I'm studying." I returned Fern's smile.

She plopped herself down in Dara's chair, her grin growing. "That sounds boring."

I laughed lightly and slipped a piece of paper between the pages of my P-chem textbook to hold my place. I knew this wouldn't be a short conversation. Over the past two weeks, Fern had been interrupting me more and more. We were often stuck together in the suite. I think the good weather kept her entertained and her options open such that she didn't usually notice me, whereas the atrocious weather of mid-winter Iowa left her with few choices.

"What would you like to do?" I asked.

"Why are you so shy?" she volleyed without warning.

I flinched, confused by the question. "Am I shy?"

She nodded, her grin still in place. "Yes. You are shy. You speak to no one who doesn't speak to you first. You never go out anywhere except the library and class and the gym. But you're not a raging killjoy psycho bitch like Beth was. You're nice...just quiet and shy."

"Well..." I considered her statement and realized she was right. "I guess I'm not great at initiating friendships."

"Why is that?"

I stared at her for a beat, thought about why I was this way. Probably my upbringing, first because of gymnastics and the hopes for my Olympic future; later because of the cancer.

More likely my reticence was because I typically enjoyed watching people more than I enjoyed actually speaking to them.

I didn't particularly want to share either of these theories with anyone. I liked my anonymity, and I liked being normal. I liked blending in.

I opened my mouth to respond with something generic, but Fern cut me off. "You are so lovely once you actually speak, not boring at all. You should be more outgoing. You are too wonderful to live so quietly. You need to get loud every once in a while."

"Okay. I'll try to do that," I promised, making a mental note to dedicate time to observing how people *get loud*.

As though reading my mind, Fern grabbed my textbook and tossed it to the floor. She reached for my hand, pulling me out of my chair.

"Excellent, let's start right now. I'll introduce you to everyone on the floor."

"I-what?" My steps faltered as I glanced down at myself. I was in my ninja star pajama bottoms and an old green wool sweater. My feet were ensconced in chunky, hand-knit wool socks. I wore no makeup, and my short brown hair was a mess.

"We'll start with the girls," she said, meeting my eyes over her shoulder and wagged her eyebrows, "then I'll introduce you to the boys."

I brought us both to a stop just as she opened the suite door. "Should I go change?"

She wrinkled her nose and snorted. "No. You're gorgeous. You're an Audrey Hepburn." She tugged on me again, successfully pulling me out of the suite.

"An Audrey Hepburn?"

"Yes, a Grace Kelly, Coco Chanel. You make everything look purposeful, like high fashion. You're..." she waved her free hand through the air theatrically, "beautiful, gorgeous, you've got *panache*, infectious...*joie de vivre! Sagesse, attrait!* There is just something about you, something wonderfully magical and ethereal."

I wrinkled my nose at her French flair and descriptions, found it discordant with reality, and decided Fern enjoyed making life dramatic and meaningful when it was really mundane, with messy hair, and dressed in ninja star pajama bottoms.

We started with several of the girls' rooms. Fern, it seemed, felt free to walk into each suite without knocking. After the first encounter, each presentation followed a predictable script.

Fern would announce herself like she was a fairy godmother, clapping her hands together to assemble all who were present—which was everyone since it was beyond freezing outside. She made introductions with flourish, putting me on the spot as the center of attention for a very short time, maybe three minutes. People would typically mention that they'd seen me or that I looked familiar; they'd ask me benign yet friendly questions about my major and where I was from. Fern would cut in, tell a scandalous joke or flirt with someone's boyfriend, and we'd be off to the next suite.

Apparently, Fern knew everyone, and everyone was really nice; but I was feeling overwhelmed by all the socialization, new faces, and new names. Regardless, even with the brief introductions, I got the feeling that this exercise was an initiation of sorts.

People would talk to me now.

I felt certain that now people would wave, stop me in the hall, ask me to join them on social outings or runs to the store. Although it seemed like such a simple thing, for the first time in my life I realized the importance of an introduction. An introduction by a mutual friend buys instant credibility, especially when the mutual friend was universally liked—as was the case with Fern.

We were leaving the fifth suite area when I collided into a solid wall. When I glanced up I realized the solid structure wasn't a wall at all. It was a boy. And this boy was studying me with unveiled interest.

"Hey, cutie." His green eyes flickered over me, quick and assessing. A lazy, blatantly flirtatious smile curved over his lips. I stepped back, lifting my chin to meet his gaze. He had long, thick blonde hair that fell to his jaw, a dazzlingly handsome face, a stocky and muscled torso—the shape of which was visible through his black T-shirt—and was inexplicably tan. He also had an abundance of blonde chest hair that was poking out through the neck of his shirt.

"Uh, hello." I gave him a polite smile and stuck my hand out. "I'm Fiona."

"Hi, *Fionaaaaah.*" He grinned widely, inadvertently drawing attention to the fact that his neck was approximately the same width as his head; his voice was maple syrup, dark and rich and too sweet to be taken seriously. "I'm Sasquatch."

"Sasquatch?"

He nodded, "That's right."

I pressed my lips together to keep from laughing because I could tell he found the nickname both sexy and flattering.

"Oh," I said and nodded. "Nice to meet you, Sasquatch."

Still holding my hand in one of his, he braced the other on the door frame above my head and loomed over me, his gaze moving up and down my body several times in a leisurely perusal.

"So," he licked his lips, "are you new here?"

"Ugh! It's you!" Fern's exclamation came from behind me, and her hands closed on my shoulders, pulling me away from...He Who Calls Himself Sasquatch.

"Oh, hey, sexy. I didn't see you there." Not missing a beat, Sasquatch leaned forward as though to give Fern a kiss.

She placed her hand over his face—her palm on his mouth—and pushed him away.

"Go away, beast." She flicked her wrist and grasped my hand, maneuvering me around Sasquatch.

"That's not what you said this morning," he called after us.

Fern spun toward him, releasing my hand and flinging me away, and—again—I collided into a solid wall. And, again, it was not a wall but the chest of a boy.

"Oph, excuse me-" I reached my hands out to steady myself as his came to my upper arms, likely with the same goal.

"You have lice in your chest hair!" I heard Fern bellow at Sasquatch some distance behind me.

I glanced up distractedly at this second boy I'd run into, wondering if he'd also be employing an aptly-titled fictional subspecies as a nickname—maybe the Yeti—and did a double-take when our eyes met.

His face was completely calm, serene, though damp and reddish on his high cheek bones and the bridge of his undeniably masculine nose. This was likely from the perspiration associated with cardiovascular exercise in cold weather. His thick, dark brown hair was standing up and in spiky disarray, like he'd just taken off a hat. His jaw was angular—his bone structure more a sharp reverse trapezoid than a square—and he was tall, at least a full foot taller than me.

But his eyes...his dark, dark brown eyes were almond shaped, and they met mine directly; they struck me at once as expressive and cautious, curious and cynical.

For no reason at all, my gaze dropped to his mouth. It held no hint of a smile, yet the first word that popped into my mind as I stared at his mouth was *generous*. He had generous lips, the bottom larger than the top, giving him the appearance of a small frown or pout. They were slightly chapped.

He smelled like snow and soap and sweat—and not rank, pungent sweat. It was a sweet, masculine smell and made my internal organs try to rearrange themselves; likely the power of male pheromones at work.

"Hello," he said, his tone dry and flat.

My eyes darted back to his, and I could feel myself blush—just a little, as I was not prone to embarrassment—at being caught staring at his mouth.

He was squinting, like a full-on Dirty Harry squint. I had the distinct impression I was being examined.

"Hi," I said, remembering myself and stepping backwards. But, rather than let me go, he took a step forward—his hands still gripping my upper arms—like we were dancing and he was matching my movements.

I blinked up at him, knowing my surprise and confusion were obvious. "What are-"

"Wait for it," he said, dipping his chin, and shifted to the side just as Sasquatch barreled down the hall past us, a spiked heel flying through the air in his wake. I became aware of a second shoe pummeling toward us, the aim very bad.

"Watch out!" I tried to move this tall, dark stranger, but he stood rigid, only flinching slightly when the shoe hit him in the head.

"Oh! Sorry, Greg!" Fern jogged past, chasing the Sasquatch and calling back to us, "That wasn't meant for you."

"It's alright; a shoe to the head is better than a shoe to the bollocks," he said, and all at once I recognized that he had an upper-crust British accent. It was diluted, but it was definitely there. His tone haughtily robotic in a way that only the British can achieve, yet a complete contradiction to the deep cadence of his voice.

He was watching their retreating forms, his face devoid

of expression, and I took the opportunity to study him further.

His form was sleek, his shoulders and arms muscled, but not overly so. His torso was slim and v-shaped. He had long legs, thick thighs, built for speed, encased in all-weather spandex. He was a runner.

I grasped that he was older than me. He had the beginnings of laugh lines or worry lines or frown lines around his eyes and mouth—I couldn't tell which. But more than that, there was an air of wisdom and experience that radiated from him, like he'd already lived a great deal.

I often find, as a cancer survivor, I tend to know when another person has lived through tragedy, prolonged physical or mental suffering. Like recognizes like, and I recognized it in this man. Usually it repelled me. I did not want to dwell on my past. These people typically wished to swap stories. I had no desire for commiseration.

But nothing about this man repelled me, nothing at all. I felt strangely and suddenly *involved*.

He glanced down, met my gaze squarely, and didn't seem at all surprised that I was ogling him.

"I'm Greg," he said matter-of-factly, releasing my arms suddenly, stepping away and directly in front of me. He lifted his gloved hand to his mouth and tugged it off with the aid of his teeth. My stare flickered to his mouth again, finding the flash of his white teeth biting his black leather glove distracting.

Before I knew it, he was holding his hand between us, offering it in a handshake.

I stared at it, not quite sure what to do.

"Shake it," he said.

Startled by the command and flustered by my inaction, I lifted my hand and fit it in his. "Yes, sorry. Hi, I'm Fiona."

He nodded once in acknowledgement, his eyes skating

over my face. "Tell me, Fiona, what do you call a female astronaut?"

I frowned at him and his question, acutely disappointed that I'd misread him. I was surprised by how upset I was, more than I should have been given the full minute we'd spent in each other's company.

College boys and their adolescent jokes, it made him less alluring and so much more...typical.

Pressing my lips together to keep from frowning, I withdrew my hand from his and shrugged, knowing my face demonstrated my lack of interest in the sudden turn of the conversation.

"I don't know, what do you call a female astronaut?" My voice mimicked the robotic quality of his.

"An astronaut, of course," he said, sounding suddenly offended—again, in that way only the British can affect—he shook his head like he was disillusioned with me. "For shame, Fiona. Your misogyny is showing."

I narrowed my eyes at him, and this time I pressed my lips together to keep from smiling. "I like that joke."

"Now female astronauts are a joke? *Tsk*." He sighed, crossing his arms, his eyes moving up and down the length of me.

"You live here," he said suddenly. "I recognize you."

I nodded, leaning against the wall and clasping my hands behind me. "Yes. I do."

"But you're a hermit."

I began to suspect that he said virtually everything in that dry tone, one employed by the innately and perpetually sarcastic, those who are too witty for their own good. It was very rapid fire, Sherlock-Holmes-esque. Usually my younger sister used that voice on my mother as a coping strategy.

One never knew if the speaker were serious or joking,

and it ran the risk of making the speaker come across as superior, arrogant, and patronizing.

But in Greg I found it to be completely charming—so far—and that (paired with his impressively lithe build, the coiled and potential power of his body, angular features, and guarded expression) made him dangerously magnetic.

"That's right," I nodded, studying him, feeling a strange electric current pass between us, "I'm a hermit."

The side of his mouth hinted at the barest of whisper of a smile, but his brown eyes betrayed only undemonstrative curiosity. "Working on any manifestos that I should know about?"

I shook my head. "None that concern you."

"But you'll keep me apprised of any that may interest me?"

"Why would you be interested in my manifestos, seeing as how I'm misogynistic?"

He glanced down the hall, obviously fighting a smile. The evidence of it made me feel triumphant for some reason, like I'd achieved something of note.

When his dark eyes turned back to me, they captured mine and dared me to look away. "I like to keep current on the latest trends, what rhetoric *you people* are spouting as truth."

"You people…?"

"Bigamists and xenophobes."

"I'm amazed by how well you know me after such a short acquaintance. Tell me, why would you want to know about my xenophobic manifestos?"

"Because sexists always have such interesting ideas."

"Sexists have interesting ideas?"

"Ideas? Yes. Ideals? No."

I scoffed, enjoying myself far too much, my heart and

stomach fluttering together, in cahoots like squealing fangirls. "Name one interesting idea that's arrived via sexism."

"Well, let's see…" His eyes narrowed again, flickered over me as though predicting my reaction to his words before he'd spoken them, "Yemeni laws state that a woman must obey her husband and must not leave home without his permission."

"And why is that interesting?" I felt a strange mixture of offended on behalf of Yemani women and incongruously curious and excited by the prospect of his answer.

"I think men will always be arrested on some level by the idea of owning their spouse, of completely possessing the woman they love, of having her unquestioning trust and obedience and admiration. But most importantly, of actually being a man that deserves it all. And I think women—though they are loathe to admit it—fundamentally want to be possessed."

"That's repugnant." I wrinkled my nose at him, trying to hide how paradoxically disturbed and bizarrely hot his words made me. "There is nothing interesting about treating women as possessions; it's dehumanizing."

"Not necessarily, not if a man treasures his possession, cherishes her, protects her—it's about ownership."

"Ownership? Possessions can be discarded, given away," I pointed out, feeling a thrill. Our conversation had become rapid fire, almost to the point of speaking over each other.

"So can people. People are discarded all the time. But if you truly own her, own her heart, if she is truly yours, abandoned to you, you cannot discard her. She is where she belongs, hence the ownership."

"Possessions don't have thoughts or feelings; they're inanimate objects."

"Ah, but women are never inanimate, not the way I do it." I ignored this comment because his tone, which remained uninflected, was at odds with the suggestiveness of his words.

"If a husband were at the whim of his wife, it would be called emasculating. But when it's the reverse, it's acceptable?"

"That's not true."

"Which part?"

"You don't like the idea of being owned? Of wholly belonging to someone?" he asked softly, his eyes warming and dipping to my neck before drifting to my lips.

"Other than to myself? No. I don't like the idea of being a possession. Do you?"

"Yes," he nodded slowly, his eyes no longer cautious. "Yes, I do quite like the idea of mutual ownership."

I sputtered, warmth suffusing my chest, twisting in my stomach, making me feel breathless. I glanced at the ceiling, then glared at him; I tried to force myself to feel the irritation I should. "I can't believe we're having this conversation."

"But you like it." Suddenly his tone changed; it was quiet, intimate, and tremendously self-assured.

I felt my grin too late; it had already split my face by the time I realized I was smiling. But his answering crooked grin and darkening eyes were worth the transparency of my expression.

He was more than fascinating, he was engaging, a curious and beautiful specimen. I found myself wanting to interact with him.

In fact, I liked him. I liked the shocking things he said, his measured offensive abrasiveness, and I let it show on my face. Furthermore I was about to admit these feelings out loud when our outrageous and flirtatious exchange was interrupted and the spell shattered.

"Greg, babe, you're not dressed yet," a girl called from several feet away, and I turned my attention towards her voice.

I had to fight the urge to gape. She was gorgeous, and she definitely wasn't a girl. Towering at almost six feet, auburn hair, whiskey-colored eyes, she had the most perfect body I'd ever seen on an actual live person.

Her gaze moved over me and settled on something between dismissive and friendly. I'd learned early on in my observations last semester that women frequently did this (sizing their fellow females up in the span of a few seconds). I used to think it was something only athletes did to other competitors.

The mysterious supermodel had clearly determined I was not a threat.

I glanced away and down at my hand-knit socks, blushing again and running my fingers through my short hair. The hot stain on my cheeks was so unlike me, and yet I welcomed the sensation, the uncomfortableness of it. This was a new experience, and I would never begrudge new experiences, not after almost losing the ability to experience anything at all.

She strolled to where we stood, a polite smile on her face, and stopped next to Greg. I kept my eyes on either her or my socks, not wanting to look at this guy I liked, whom I thought I'd been flirting with. But in reality, he was likely just making sociable—albeit odd—conversation.

"We have twenty minutes before we have to be there." She paused just long enough to give him a kiss then wipe away the lipstick with her thumb. She turned to me and gave me a wave, "Hi, I'm Vanessa."

I returned her wave and friendly politeness with a sincere smile. "Hi, I'm Fiona. I live on that side." I pointed down the hall.

"Did you just move in?"

Greg answered before I could, "No. She's a xenophobic hermit who writes chauvinistic manifestos."

Vanessa shook her head, her smile growing confused, and she hit him on the shoulder. "You're weird."

My gaze flickered to Greg's, and I found him watching me with some inscrutable expression. I ignored it, pushed it from my mind, chalked the current of electricity I'd felt up to my seldom-used imagination and likely one-sided attraction.

Fern was right. I needed to actually interact with people more; observation was only so helpful. I needed to get out there and live.

"Well, I have to get back to studying." I said this to Vanessa, giving her another wave. "I'm sure I'll see you around."

"It was nice to meet you." She returned the wave and fit her hand in Greg's.

I turned without meeting his eyes and crossed my arms as I shuffled down the hall, greeting two girls I'd met earlier during Fern's grand tour. I ignored the lingering tightness in my chest and heated flush of my skin.

***

THAT NIGHT I slept in Fern's spare bed as Dara and Hivan were still going at it, obviously having made up at some point.

I felt an odd sense of happiness and peace.

When I hit eighteen the summer before college, I began to suspect there was something wrong with me. The last time I'd felt anything resembling a crush or interest in a boy had been during the fifth grade, before I'd been pulled out of school for a regimen of gymnastics and private tutors.

When I was diagnosed with cancer at fourteen, crushes and boys and the future ceased to hold meaning or feel real. By the time I was in recovery, academics held all of my focus. I was determined to leave my parents' house.

Even so, during the course of my entire life, I'd never been aware or had an inkling that someone was attracted to me.

I thought of Sasquatch and his blatant leering. Even though he was an obvious player, it cheered me; his antics made me laugh lightly into my pillow.

Since I'd gone into remission, I'd often wondered if I was ugly. I would stop in front of mirrors and survey my face, shape, and general appearance.

I decided that I wasn't ugly.

I had big brown eyes with long, thick lashes. I had a nice, normal nose. I had a nice mouth full of straight white teeth and framed by perfectly adequate lips. My face was oval and my skin free of blemishes. My dark brown hair was acceptable, still short due to the years of radiation.

No. I wasn't ugly.

Nor was I an ugly person. I was a nice person. And I was smart. I was normal.

My thoughts turned to Greg and Vanessa, how lovely they looked together, how right and beautiful, and I felt a surge of happiness and hope. The momentary interest and attraction I'd felt for Greg was a good thing, something I should treasure as proof that I was alive and my heart still beat and air still filled my lungs.

Haughty and handsome Greg may have been meant for the stunning and friendly Vanessa. However, given the fact that my heart still beat and air still filled my lungs, surely there was someone out there for me. Now I just needed to stop watching people and actually talk to them.

Part 2: Knock, knock...NINJA!

"NO, IT'S A matter of decency."

"And who decides what is decent?"

I slowed my steps as I approached the dorm kitchen, especially when I thought I recognized the second speaker's voice. Without realizing what I was doing, I stopped and waited for the conversation to continue. I didn't have to wait long.

"You're being purposefully obtuse." A woman spoke; she sounded extremely frustrated.

"I'm not. I'm merely pointing out that one person's decent is another person's indecent," came the laconic—almost bored—response. The speaker was Greg.

My body stiffened, and I clutched the washing bin closer to my chest. Within were dishes too dirty for a simple rinse in the bathroom sink. I felt a slight disturbance in the cadence of my heart and realized I was holding my breath. I forced myself to breathe out. I rolled my eyes at my bizarre behavior and willed my feet to move.

They didn't move.

"That's bull," she said, sounding disgusted. "You can't tell me that harming animals is okay!"

"I can tell you whatever I please. I can tell you that Shaquille O'Neal is my cousin and that James here is having sexual relations with his hotdog bun. It might not be true, but I can say it."

"Hey, leave me and my bun out of it!" Presumably this objection came from the aforementioned James.

I pressed my lips together to keep from grinning, belatedly realizing I'd been eavesdropping. Shaking myself, I charged forward and into the kitchen. I wasn't going to turn into a creepy lurker just because I found

Greg interesting…okay, more than interesting. Really, I shouldn't have been thinking about him at all. He had a girlfriend.

"Get back to the point. Do you or do you not believe that having sex with animals is wrong? Do you believe that it's cruelty to animals? Yes or no."

I glanced around the room as I entered, nodding to several people who looked up from the debate, a few girls and guys I recognized from my tour of the dorms and subsequent social interactions. I counted almost thirty people crowded in the kitchen, most sitting on the floor, their attention rapt on Greg and a tall girl with long blonde dreadlocks. I recognized her as Simone, political science and women's studies senior, and she was giving Greg a look that would incinerate most people.

Greg looked untroubled and amused.

"That's not the point at all," he said. "And if it were the point, I counter with the fact that farmers and veterinarians frequently lend a helping masturbatory hand in the worthwhile cause of animal husbandry."

"That's a different matter entirely. The horse isn't being raped."

Greg's eyes flickered to mine, and he did a double take; his amused expression wavered, his eyebrows pulling low for an instant. But he turned his attention back to Simone. I watched him gather a deep breath, his eyes blinking three or four times as though he was trying to bring her back into focus. I ambled to the vacant sink and washed my dishes; but I kept the water pressure low so I could listen to the debate.

"Hello? Greg…the difference with animal husbandry is the absence of rape."

"Ah, well then," he cleared his throat, "what about the great demand for horse on human pornography—yes, that's right, videos of horses having sexual relations with women. A horse going on a human ride, saddle optional, of course."

This was met with some groans and some laughter. I cringed, tried not to laugh, failed, and cringed—feeling guilty for laughing.

"Ugh! You are so disgusting! I can't believe you're laughing-" Simone glared at several of the spectators, her hands balling into fists. She was obviously seething.

"Is the horse being raped because it's a vagina and not a hand? Or is it the human male penis that you find so distasteful? Regardless," he held up his hands and raised his voice before she could interrupt, "the point of this discussion isn't whether bestiality is appropriate or disgusting. The point I am attempting to make, and obviously quite clumsily, is that it is not possible to *give* offense if there is not a party to *take* offense."

"That is so wrong-"

"No. It is so right!"

I glanced up, surprised by the sudden vehemence in Greg's voice, and found him frowning. All of his earlier amusement replaced with a fierceness I couldn't quite reconcile with his horrid joking. The room fell completely silent. The only noise was the slight sound of water from the faucet.

He was gritting his teeth. "You think of bunny rabbits being butchered for fur coats and sheep farmers taking their pleasure from livestock, but you think nothing of actual atrocities, genocide, hundreds of thousands of people murdered or left to starve or forgotten. This country raises millions—if not billions—of dollars for cuddly cats and dogs, yet we do nothing to ease the suffering of and subjugation of those in third world countries. You think bestiality is offensive? I find you and your defective priorities offensive. You *give* me offense because I am inclined to *take* it."

Simone stared at him as though he'd slapped her. It was a terrible moment. On one hand, he was right. But he was also very, very wrong. For these impressionable minds that had gathered in the kitchen, it was a life-altering moment, and something within me demanded that I speak up, challenge him before these young people left this room feeling like efforts toward righting wrongs—all wrongs—were futile.

"You are correct," I said, turning off the faucet, ignoring how my heart leapt to my throat.

Greg's eyes cut to me. He was scowling. "Of course I'm correct-"

"You are also incorrect."

His forehead wrinkled, plain surprise flickering over, then arresting his expression. My heart was thudding in my chest, and my ears were ringing because he was intimidating. But I'd long ago learned how to surmount intimidation and fear. His cold regard frightened me, but I was more brave than he was scary.

"Really," he drawled, his eyes narrowing, his mouth curving in a slight smirk. "I am so very interested in learning of my deficiencies."

"That's a lie," I said plainly, wiping off my hands with a towel. "But, as sarcasm is an effective technique when debating, I'll allow it."

"You'll allow it," he stated, his voice impassive, monotone.

"Yes, I will. Even though sarcasm is beneath you. But I digress, as your lack of sincerity isn't the point."

"What is your point?"

"I agree. Without someone to take offense, one cannot give offense. That stated, values are important. Ethics are important. Morality, holding truths sacred, is important."

"Ah, but whose truths do we hold sacred?"

I shook my head and smiled at him, seeing that he was attempting to lead me down the same path he'd just led Simone. "No, no, no. That way leads to ruin and red herrings."

His eyes lost some of their cold edge, and his lips twisted to the side fighting a reluctant smile.

"The point I debate is not whose truths or ideology are superior. The point I debate is that each of us needs an ideology. We all need something to fight for, to believe in, to hold sacred. Simone-" I motioned to her with my hand, "is an animal-rights activist. No one should be belittling her good work, because she is doing good work."

His smirk fell away, and he blatantly stared, assessing. He opened his mouth to speak, and I held up my hands to stop him.

"I know what you're going to say."

"Is that so?"

"Yes. Well, maybe not the precise words, but you're going to say something sarcastic, cutting; perhaps it'll be witty or even funny. I challenge you to answer my next question without sarcasm."

His gaze narrowed again.

One of the boys chimed in, "I don't think Greg can go more than a minute without sarcasm. It might kill him."

A few people laughed. I kept my eyes on Greg. He wasn't smiling.

"Fine. What's the question?"

"Do you hold anything sacred?"

He paused, maybe searching his mind to determine if I'd asked a trick question; finally, he nodded once. "Of course."

"What good work do you do? How do you fight for what you hold sacred?"

Greg blinked as if he were startled by the question. All at once, his gaze turned thunderous.

I almost took a step back, but I didn't. I held my ground. "You give *me* offense, and I take it. I take offense to the fact that you would stand here and belittle Simone's beliefs and her work to correct what she feels are grave wrongs when you take no action to fight for your beliefs. It is one thing to compare or even belittle sacred truths when both parties are working toward rectifying wrongs. But it is quite another to rail against a person who is doing something when you do nothing."

Greg's eyes flashed, and, though I didn't know him very well, I sensed he was very close to losing his temper. I braced myself, waiting for the storm. I was good at this. My mother was a screamer. She communicated via threats and intimidation, all shouted at maximum volume.

But his anger didn't come.

He closed his eyes, his chin falling to his chest for maybe three seconds, and when he lifted his head his gaze was cool, calm, collected.

"I cede the point," he said evenly, almost cheerfully, giving me a half smile that did not reach his eyes. "You are, of course, right. What good are convictions if you don't fight for them? They're nothing."

I gave him a sideways glare, waiting for the other shoe to drop, for the acerbic remark.

He continued, "I acknowledge the superiority of your argument and would like to offer you the services of my horse in recompense, if you feel inclined to...take or give a ride."

Ah...there it is.

Of course, several people laughed. Simone bristled.

I shrugged, tossing my thumb over my shoulder. "I'll have to take a rain check as I have dishes to do."

"Perhaps after?"

"No, thanks." I strolled back to the sink. "Afterwards I need to give my fish a bath."

A number of students chuckled or smirked, and I was relieved when new conversations were initiated within the group, a few people wondering out loud if anyone was up for playing Mario Kart. Obviously they'd tired of the ethics debate.

Meanwhile, I turned my attention back to my dishes and found that my hands were shaking, just a very little but enough that I noticed. I finished the dishes in record time, feeling Greg's gaze on me but not inclined to meet it. I wiped the area around the sink and decided to dry my dishes in my room rather than loiter in the kitchen any longer.

My pace was quicker than I liked as I exited the room, but I forced myself to slow to a stroll when I reached the hall. I had no reason to run away...or so I told myself.

"Fiona."

I tensed, my steps faltering, halting at the sound of my name in Greg's accent. I turned, giving Greg my profile. He was striding purposefully toward me. His jaw was set, his gaze half-lidded; as he drew closer I saw the muscle at his temple tick.

I gave him the best friendly and interested expression I could muster. "Hey...Greg."

He stopped; his eyes, guarded and measured, flickered over me and rested on the tub of clean dishes I was holding. "Let me carry these back for you."

Without waiting for me to acquiesce, he took the tub from my grip and preceded me down the hall toward my room. He entered my suite. I was several paces behind and was surprised that he knew which door was mine.

I found him hovering just inside the entrance, his gaze

moving over Fern's books and papers, Beth's vacant space, Dara's desk and mine. He set the tub down on what used to be Beth's empty stretch of table and turned to face me. His jaw was still tight, his generous lips a stiff line.

I was struck with the notion that he was tormented, that something plagued him. I didn't know how to address it; I didn't know if I should.

I offered, "Do you, uh, do you want something to drink?"

"You're wrong about me."

I lifted my right eyebrow in surprise and waited for him to continue. When he didn't, I asked the obvious question, "How am I wrong about you?"

"I've fought for my beliefs; I've fought for them most of my life. But the fight yields nothing. What you did, what you said to those kids-"

"Kids?" I asked, incredulous, interrupting him. If the assorted upper classmen arranged in the kitchen were kids, then I was an infant.

He ignored me, and as he spoke his voice became increasingly dispassionate, "-I understand why you did it, but it's a band-aid on a wound that festers. People fill their minds with trivial things because they cannot face horrible truths."

I studied him and saw that he was agitated. Behind his droll mask and irreverent quips, I perceived a boy—no, a man—who was struggling. I had the overwhelming urge to ease his struggle. I started to lift my hands, then quickly balled them into fists at my sides. Comforting Greg was not my place.

Instead, I gently offered, "Not everyone is capable of fighting the great fights. Not everyone is brave and strong and powerful. Let people have their causes. Allow them their victories, when victories can be had, without begrudging the wrongs that they right. Attending to injustice, no matter how small, is always a worthy cause."

His hands were on his hips, and he was giving me a sideways glare, examining me, though his mouth was curved in a somnolent smile. He studied me for a very long moment, and I allowed him to do so, even though I sensed he was bursting with restless energy.

As well, I became increasingly aware of the strange current building. The atmosphere grew charged and heavy; although I reasoned he was likely unaware and/or immune to it. I felt my attraction for him increasing, ballooning, even given his abrasive comments in the kitchen. I should've run in the other direction. Instead I found myself wanting to soothe him.

Also, a tortured Greg was so devastatingly handsome it made my throat tight and my chest hurt. Mostly, I just wanted to touch him.

But I didn't.

He huffed a small laugh, breaking the tension, and glanced at the ceiling. "You make too much sense."

I smiled, my eyes widening at the compliment. "I know. It's a curse."

He crossed his arms over his chest, pulling the sleeves of his navy blue long-sleeved T-shirt tight over his muscled shoulders. It took all my willpower not to look at his neck. His skin tone was a radiant olive, perma-tanned. It looked like it would be warm to the touch. I crossed my arms.

"Just stop it," he said, his tone now dry, though I could tell he was teasing.

"Okay. I'll stop being well reasoned."

"Good. Be a fruitcake."

"No one likes fruitcakes."

"I do."

"You're the only one."

"I should be enough," he said.

I narrowed a single eye at him, scrunching one side of my face and teased him back. "No. Not nearly enough. I require legions of adoring fans."

He nodded and this time couldn't master his smile. "I sense that about you. You strike me as needy and narcissistic."

"You're very perceptive. I require constant praise for my misogynistic manifestos."

He laughed, and it was such a wonderful sound my heart gave a stupid leap in response. I wanted to press my hand against my chest, but instead I held my breath.

The moment of levity ended with a smiling staring contest that soon transitioned into an extremely awkward non-smiling staring contest. His gaze moved over my face, his eyes a tad unfocused. I fought the urge to fidget (and won). Instead I stood perfectly still and gave myself this moment, with him, alone.

Then it was over.

Greg shook his head and pulled his hand through his longish hair. He rushed to the door. "I should go. I have puppies to club and kittens to drown…someplace."

He left.

I stood completely still for several long moments, staring at the place he'd hurriedly vacated. The small suite area felt abruptly enormous without him in it. I reminded myself that he belonged to someone else. I would never show any sign of outward interest, but I would look. I would admire.

And I would do my very best not to covet.

***

I HAD A date! In February…on Valentine's Day.

His idea.

His name was Mark, but I'd nicknamed him "Legs" because he had the nicest legs, and, despite the fact that it was snowing outside, he always wore basketball shorts. I wasn't complaining or questioning the sanity of this because it meant I got to look at his legs during class. Though I could have nicknamed him "Smiles" or "Blue Eyes" or "Blondie" because he had a magnificent smile and the loveliest blue eyes and the prettiest blond hair.

We met in art history class shortly after Fern had made me realize that I had a bad habit of not smiling or talking to people. I stopped watching people and started meeting people's gazes, smiling at them. It made a huge difference.

Legs sat two seats down from mine in the giant lecture hall. On my first day back in class after Fern's grand tour of the dorms, I smiled at him. He smiled, then moved two seats closer to me, and introduced himself.

Mark was eighteen, a farmer's son, and the first person in his family to go to college. He wanted to be a civil engineer. He was really very good looking and friendly and sweet. He asked me if I'd like to join his art history study group—which I did—and then asked later in the week if I wanted to grab coffee—which I did.

Over coffee he asked me out. I said yes. He set the date, and we made plans.

Mark gave me a tiny excited flutter in my stomach, nothing like the overwhelming magnetic pull I'd experienced with Greg, but I was looking forward to the date. I wasn't looking for anything long term. I wanted to experience something new.

Shortly after Mark asked me out, but before our date, I was asked out for coffee by a guy I'd smiled at in my P-chem class. His name was Jefferson, and he was adorable. I'd said yes but then later questioned this decision since I had a date scheduled with Mark.

This was also a new experience. So I sought out Fern to ask her what I should do. I tried several rooms of the girls I'd met and become friendly with over the last few weeks; one of them told me to try Greg's room as Fern and Greg had political science together and typically studied after class.

My first instinct was to wait for Fern in my suite area rather than go to Greg's room. Just the thought of going to Greg's room gave me a wild feeling, hot and flushed, anxious. The last time I'd spent time with him, after the great kitchen debate, he'd left my room suddenly with a hurried and fictional excuse. I hadn't spoken to him since...

I finally shook myself out of my reticence.

He was just a boy. He was harmless. He had a girlfriend who was gorgeous and sociable. I would calibrate my smiles and interactions to friendship or acquaintance level. No big deal.

Armed with my altruistic pragmatism, I marched to Greg's. His suite was on the opposite end of the hall from mine, thirty doors separating us. This realization made me feel better for some reason.

I was prepared to knock but the suite door was open: I heard Fern's voice as I approached. I decided I'd poke my head around the corner, interrupt briefly, ask Fern to come find me when she was finished, and then leave.

I poked my head around the corner and, thankfully, found Fern facing the door. Greg's back was to me. She looked up instantly and gave me a smile.

"Hey, Fiona. You're out and about."

"Yes, I don't want to interrupt. Just real fast, when you're finished can you give me a few minutes? I need your advice."

Greg had turned in his seat, and I could feel his eyes on

me; I glanced down at him and gave him a head nod and a tight smile of acknowledgement.

"What kind of advice?" he asked, his tone as dry as ever.

"Just girl stuff." I waved his question away then turned my attention back to Fern. "So I'll see you later?"

"Girl stuff? Sounds exciting." Fern's eyes widened, and she rubbed her hands together.

Meanwhile, Greg stood and pulled a chair over from the other side of the suite. I was momentarily distracted by the sight of him in boot cut jeans, bare feet, and a plain white T-shirt. He was so tall and lean and delicious. My preoccupation with his body was likely why, when he grabbed my wrist as he returned and placed me in the seat he'd just vacated, I didn't object.

"I'm excellent with girl stuff," he said, taking the new seat so that both he and Fern faced me, as though I were about to be interviewed. "Ask any girl, they'll all tell you how good I am with the girl stuff."

"I, uh…" I turned to stand, not sure what to do.

But then Fern placed her hand on my knee to stay my retreat, "No, he really is. He's fantastic with the girl stuff. Just think of him as one of the girls." Her eyes flickered to him, moving up and down his body. He returned this perusal with a sardonic eyebrow lift.

"Well," she amended, "think of him as a girl in a man's body. He's got the brain of a woman."

He nodded. "Yes. Shrewd. Calculating. Resilient. Ruthless."

I found myself rolling my lips between my teeth to keep from beaming at him. It occurred to me that this would be good practice. Being around Greg and tempering my reactions to him would help me navigate similar situations in the future.

Greg leaned forward, his elbows on his knees—he

looked too big for the chair—and with a
delivery, he said, "Just tell Aunty Gregina all abo

Both Fern and I laughed, and I shook my
narrowing my eyes at him. Though his face was sol
his dark eyes were warm and teasing. I imagined he had
unbeatable poker face.

"Fine, here's the story," I sighed, still giving him a
suspicious glare—something I'd seen Fern do to her legion
of boys who were just friends on a number of occasions—
then moved my attention back to Fern. I was having
trouble looking at him and forming complete sentences.
He made me feel warm and disoriented. "You know Mark,
from my art history class?"

Fern nodded at me, then supplied for Greg, "He's taking
Fiona out on a date on Valentine's Day."

Greg shifted in his seat. "He's your boyfriend."

I shook my head, allowing my attention to stray to him
just for a second. "No, it's our first date."

"On Valentine's Day." His matter-of-fact tone held a
hint of disbelief.

"That's right, so the thing is-"

"You should cancel it. Only a nutter takes a girl out for
the first date on Valentine's Day. Or a pedophile."

Fern hit him on the shoulder. "Greg!"

He rubbed his shoulder like she'd hurt him, "What? You
want our darling Fiona to go on a date with a pedophile?"

"Mark is not a pedophile." Her voice became squeaky
because she was shouting.

"How do you know? Are you well acquainted with the
local chapter of child molesters? Have them over for tea?"

"You are so awful." She shook her head, though she
looked like she was valiantly fighting the urge to laugh.

"Perhaps you supply them with the candy for their

burst out laughing, "Oh my God, lieve you're making jokes about

1e laughing? I'm the one trying _gling body bits with the local _...-boy-love."

...c *was* awful. He was irreverent and offensive and abrasive, and, for some strange reason which should have alarmed me, I found him completely enchanting. Perhaps the shock value appealed to me because my entire life had been so sheltered. Or perhaps I was twisted and wrong in some way.

Whatever the reason, his appalling comedy routine, delivered with a dry superiority, made him even more attractive.

I was definitely twisted and wrong.

"Just...just," Fern held up her hand in front of his face, "just shut it, and let Fiona ask her question." Then she turned to me, "Please, continue."

"Okay..." I glanced between the two of them. Greg appeared to be completely at ease and all things attentive and serious. However, I sensed mischief lay just below the surface.

"So, the question is about Jefferson."

"Jefferson?" Fern and Greg asked at the same time, though he sounded a tad alarmed.

Fern gave Greg a quelling look and leaned forward an inch. "Who is Jefferson?"

"Jefferson is a guy in my P-Chem class."

"P-Chem? Aren't you a freshman?" Greg asked.

I nodded once, allowing myself to admire the shape of his lips and jaw as I answered, "Yes, but I took the AP exams for most of my prerequisites."

"So your major is…?"

"Stop interrupting, Greg." Fern rolled her eyes.

"It's okay. My major is electrical engineering."

His gaze narrowed as his eyes flickered over me again, as though seeing me for the first time. "What other classes are you taking?"

"Well, um…differential equations, P-chem, vector calculus, dynamics, and art history."

He stared at me, his expression plainly betraying his surprise. I met his startled glare directly, waiting for him to make a comment. Instead he continued to study me in silence.

Fern drew my attention back to her by snapping her fingers. "Back to Jefferson from P-chem."

"Oh, yes. Well, Jefferson has asked me out for coffee. My question is, is it wrong to go out for coffee with Jefferson if I'm going on a date with Mark?"

"I knew a Jefferson," Greg mumbled, studying his fingernails. "He used to bugger animals, probably still does. I wonder if it's the same Jefferson…"

Fern growled, her eyes slicing to him, then back to me. She gave me a small smile. "No, it's not wrong at all. You and Mark aren't established enough to be exclusive. Until you become exclusive with a person, you can date as many other guys as you like."

"Just don't have sex with any of them." Greg's words were anxious, drawing both mine and Fern's attention.

His mouth was curved downward at the edges, and his eyes no longer appeared teasing. He cleared his throat, studied his hands, then lifted his gaze to Fern's.

"Just until…until she's exclusive with someone," he explained.

Fern gave him an irritated flick of her wrist—I'd noticed she used her hands often in conversation—and turned back to me. "Don't listen to him. Sex up as many boys as you like."

I feigned a light chuckle. A girl in my art history study group did this often when she became uncomfortable, hoping to lighten a suddenly strained mood. "Yeah, I don't think I'll be sexing anyone up for a while."

Fern's smile was wistful, and her hazel eyes took on an almost motherly glint. "Oh, that's right. You've never been kissed, have you?"

Everything went silent and time stood still.

My heart stuttered, skipped a beat; it was tripping on mortification and overwhelming embarrassment.

I had no idea what to do, how to react, how to behave. I'd never experienced or witnessed this type of situation before.

I kept thinking, *Now he knows...now he knows I've never been kissed...now he thinks I'm a freak.*

All I knew was that I wanted to fall into a black hole and disappear. An unpleasant hot and clammy sensation spread over my skin; I was sweating for no reason. I felt Greg's eyes on me, and they were like two laser beams burning into my skull. My scalp itched.

"That's right," I said, swallowing thickly, nodding jerkily, forcing a smile. "Not yet." In a fit of desperation, I decided to add self-deprecating cheerfulness as I gave them two thumbs up... Two incredibly awkward thumbs up. "But I have high hopes for Valentine's Day."

Instinct told me to run, to escape, so I did.

I stood suddenly, pushing the chair to the side to clear my path, and darted out of the room as I called, "Well, thanks for your advice; that's what I needed."

I fled back to my room, and I didn't know why. Some

sense of urgency spurred my steps; my throat was tight, and I felt like I was going to cry. I didn't know what was wrong with me.

I'd experienced embarrassment before, the frustration associated with failing in front of thousands of spectators and millions of TV viewers. As an Olympic contender I'd learned how to move past failure, put it out of my mind, focus on the next goal, the next competition. Obsessing about mistakes was counterproductive to success. I always learned from my mistakes. Then I moved on.

But this was different. This horrible feeling was due to an audience of one and wasn't about failure or a mistake; it wasn't about something I could control. There was nothing to analyze for future improvement. I felt irrationally embarrassed and melancholy and wretched, like I'd been kicked repeatedly.

Try as I might, I couldn't bring myself to feel grateful for this new experience.

***

TWO DAYS BEFORE Valentine's Day, I came home to find Dara's side of the room packed into suitcases. She explained that she was going to go home for a week. Things were getting too crazy with her and Hivan; she said she needed a break.

I helped Dara take her bags down to the car and gave her a hug before she departed, fresh tears in her blue eyes. She was a really nice girl, and I felt sad for her.

I wandered back to my suite but was stopped in the hall by a few girls on the floor.

"You're Dara's roommate, right?" a tall blonde asked, indicating with her head toward my room.

I nodded. "That's right."

"Is it true? Did she go home to have an abortion?"

I stared askance at this stranger, too shocked by the

audacity of the question to process whether or not it might be true. "I- I don't- I mean, no. I should say, not that-"

"Gail, don't be such a bitch. It's none of our business." This comment came from a petite redhead.

"I just asked a question." The one called Gail held her hands up as though defending herself. Now I recognized her; Fern had told me during our grand tour weeks ago that Gail was the floor gossip. She meant well but couldn't help herself from getting into everyone's business.

"It's nothing like that," the redhead continued, her expression stern. "Dara just needs a break from her prick boyfriend."

"Did they break up?" Gail's eyes became wide, searching.

"Do you ever stop?" The redhead shook her head at Gail's antics, then turned to me. "I'm Maddie. I think we met before. Dara says you're the sweetest."

I smiled at Maddie and shook her hand. "Nice to meet you."

"I'm telling you, there is something going around, some kind of Valentine's Day bad mojo. Everyone is breaking up." Gail delivered this with squinted eyes, pursed lips, and a head nod for emphasis.

"Oh, yeah..." A blonde girl, approximately my height who'd been silent thus far, waved her hands in the air excitedly. (I remembered her name was Sarah or Silvia or something like that.) "That's right! Did you all hear about Vanessa and Greg?"

I stilled, but my heart took off, my wide eyes betraying my avid interest, and the words were out of my mouth before I could catch them, "No, what happened?"

I knew I would dislike myself later for gossiping, but for now I indulged with the hunger of a voracious animal. My pulse doubled in the three seconds it took for her to share the news.

She glanced over both her shoulders then leaned in, lowering her voice to a whisper. "He broke up with her last week. She's devastated."

My heart soared then dipped, and I felt at once elated and miserable about my elation.

Since our last interaction, Greg and I had passed each other a few times in the hall. Usually he was with Vanessa, and the three of us would exchange polite greetings— though sometimes he would ask about my manifestos and beleaguer me with pointed glares. I would laugh good-naturedly and give a noncommittal shrug, feeling embarrassed and uncomfortable each time.

Last week I saw him at a party. Now that I'd succumbed to Fern's overtures and pressure to socialize, I'd gone to my very first party, and Greg was there. Upon seeing him, I promptly spun on my heel and maneuvered to a different room. I left shortly thereafter, unable to relax.

If I knew he was going to be part of a group gathering, I didn't go.

If I saw him on campus, I walked the other way.

I'd spotted him at the gym several times and took an alternate route to my destination.

I was outright avoiding him. Our short exchanges had yielded the strongest attraction and connection I'd felt for another person, and it felt heavy with significance. Avoiding Greg felt like the smart thing to do if I wanted to find a connection with someone else.

As well, the thought of facing him again now that he knew I'd never even been kissed filled me with metric tons of dread.

"Oh my God, why? What happened?" Gail nearly squealed the question, grabbing the other blonde girl's hand as though the news might make her lose her balance.

"I don't know the particulars, only that Vanessa has been crying nonstop, and Greg was the one who broke up with her. I don't think she saw it coming."

"She's gorgeous." Maddie said this wistfully, her eyes losing focus. "If she can't keep a boyfriend, then what hope do the rest of us have?"

"Don't be so dramatic, Maddie." Gail scrunched her nose. "Maybe she didn't know how to keep her man happy. Greg is...well, that's a lot of man right there. Vanessa might be beautiful, but beauty fades. Greg knows that."

The other blonde chimed in, "Yeah, she had her chance. They've been dating for over a year."

I felt my eyebrows jump at the calculating look in their eyes. It seemed that I wasn't the only one who'd appreciated Greg from afar.

The absurdity of the situation hit me abruptly and I almost laughed out loud at myself. I'd received the news of Greg and Vanessa's break up with the same greedy, hungry appetite as any girl who likes a boy with a girlfriend. In my fantasies, the fact that Greg no longer had a girlfriend might mean that I had a chance with him.

I looked around at the starry eyes of these three girls, all imagining the same fantasy, all physically beautiful in their own way, and I recognized that reality painted a very different picture. But more than that, I didn't like what I saw: three lovely girls celebrating the heartbreak of a fellow female.

My competition days were long over. Besides, I'd never been a person who could feel joy at the sorrow of another.

I chose to embrace the feelings of melancholy instead, that a nice girl like Vanessa had apparently had her heart broken.

I *tsked*. "I hope she's okay. I've only met her a few

times, but she seems really nice. Does she have someone to talk to?"

All three of them stared at me. After a brief moment each of them had the decency to look various shades of ashamed.

"Uh...yeah. Vanessa and her roommate are really tight. I'm sure Carly will help her deal."

"That's good." I nodded, then repeated something Fern said often, "Girls need to stick together, support each other."

Gail looked me up and down, like I was strange and she was suddenly uncomfortable.

"That's right," she said, then took a step back. "I have laundry to do. Come on, Maddie."

Maddie gave me a shy grin, and the three girls disappeared down the hall.

I watched them go, then turned to my own suite and shut the door behind me. I was greeted by rare silence. It was Thursday. Fern was at class then would be gone until all hours as she had no classes on Fridays. Dara was gone, and stillness replaced the constant soundtrack of her breakups and makeups with Hivan.

For the first time in months, I had a quiet evening to myself.

I would not think about Greg.

I would not think about Greg.

I would not think about Greg...

I wished I could talk to my sister.

I decided to take a nap.

***

I WAS WOKEN up by a knock on the door. My eyes were blurry, unfocused, as I squinted at my nightstand. When it finally came into view, my alarm clock told me it was just past 11:30 p.m. I sat up, rubbing my eyelids, and staggered to a standing position.

"Who is it?" I called, giving myself a moment to find my balance, my voice raspy with sleep.

"How is it possible that you've never been kissed?"

I sucked in a breath, suddenly quite awake, and I'm sure my heart stopped.

It was Greg's voice, and he sounded…different. His accent was thicker, more pronounced, though his speech was slower.

"Fiona?" he called when I remained silent.

I swallowed, finding my throat and mouth very dry, and managed to croak, "Greg?"

"Open the door, would you?" came his muffled reply.

I took a step toward the door, but then stopped, hopping from foot to foot. "Greg, what are you doing here?"

"I live here."

"No, not in the building. What are you doing in my suite? It's almost midnight."

"I'm quite drunk," he said. Despite his imbibed state, his tone was still flat and matter-of-fact. "And because I'm intoxicated, coming to your room in the middle of the night feels like the only thing to do."

I shook my head, searching my room, my hands balling into fists. I didn't know what to do. I didn't know him, not really. We'd spoken only a handful of times. Opening the door to a very tall, very strong, and very drunk almost stranger in the middle of the night felt like the beginning of every cautionary tale young girls are told.

"Maybe you should go sleep it off," I said, crossing my arms over my chest.

I heard a thud; something hit the door. I suspected it was his forehead.

He sounded pained when he said, "That's a good idea. Send me away. Very wise of you."

I flexed my fingers then balled them into fists again, waiting for some sound marking his retreat and mentally mourning my good sense. My brain liked this guy, my body liked this guy, and my heart was beyond infatuated with him.

But my intrinsic sensible nature wouldn't allow me to do anything stupid. In all things I've always been well-reasoned.

Then he said, obviously having not moved from his spot at the door, "I want to be your first kiss."

I rocked on my feet, the already dark room dimming and spinning slightly, and I pressed my hand to my violently fluttering stomach.

"Greg…" I breathed his name reflexively, shocked, and found myself at a loss for words.

My silence didn't seem to matter to him because he said, sounding quite tortured, "I want to be your first everything."

I reached my hand out and leaned against the dresser to my right, steadying myself.

Greg continued speaking to the door, his voice laced with an edge of frustration, "And it makes no fucking sense because I don't even know you, but I can't stop thinking about you. I saw you during the first week of class last semester, and, Christ, you're gorgeous, but you're so…different, sad…ethereal. You walked right past me for months, but I saw you every time. Though you hide it, I see the sorrow in you…or maybe you don't know…"

My mind was reeling. I didn't know which part of his speech to focus on first. But he didn't give me any time to think about or react to his confession.

"We were in English composition together last semester,

but you don't know that because you never saw me." Something soft connected with the door, and I felt certain he'd placed his palm against it. "I sat seven rows behind you and talked myself out of approaching you every bloody day because I had a girlfriend, and I owed her more than that, more than feigning friendship with you when that's not what I wanted. And I'm a bastard for staying with Vanessa when I'm thinking about someone else. Did I mention that I'm very drunk?"

I nodded, then realized he couldn't see me, and said, "Yes. You mentioned you are drunk."

"Don't let me in," he said, his voice back to its emotionless baseline. "I might ravish you or force you into a hasty, unsuitable marriage."

I choked a laugh then covered my face with my hands, finding my cheeks hot and flushed.

"I'm leaving now," he said, then I heard him mumble something like, "...after making a total ass of myself."

My heart jumped, like it wanted to leave my chest, and I took an automatic step toward the door. "Greg..." I searched for words but felt completely overwhelmed and lost. Finally I said, "Come back when you're sober."

He was quiet for several seconds, so quiet I feared that he'd already left, but then he said, "Promise me you won't kiss anyone between now and tomorrow morning."

I rolled my eyes and grinned, glancing at the ceiling. "I'll make no promises until I speak to sober Greg."

"Then I'll sleep out here to keep would-be suitors away, as well as any other stalkers who wake you up in the middle of the night with declarations of unending devotion."

"Don't sleep out there." I didn't want him cramped and uncomfortable on the floor. I hated it when other people were uncomfortable; I couldn't be comfortable if I knew someone else was uncomfortable.

"Then let me sleep in there. Your roommate is gone, yes?"

That was a bad idea…it was a bad idea that sounded really, really great.

"No." I tried to force resolve into my tone. "Absolutely not."

"Ah, well…it was worth a try. Likely would have worked if you were anyone else." I pictured his crooked smile, a smile I could hear in his words. Even drunk he knew he was witty and virtually irresistible.

"Go to your room, and go to sleep." I almost succeeded in sounding convinced.

"Fine," he said. "But I'm not one of those drunks who feels ashamed of their behavior the next day…granted I might pretend to forget everything that's just happened, but I'll never feel ashamed."

I sensed that he'd moved away from the door, and some instinct had me crossing to it, touching the doorknob.

"Fiona?"

I closed my eyes, imagining his face. My heart gave another painful tug. "Yes, Greg?"

"Tell me you feel it, too."

I swallowed, hesitated, though I immediately knew what he meant. Despite his drunken leap of faith, I found the prospect of admitting anything of my own feelings to this man enormously frightening, another new experience.

With Mark and Jefferson admitting my *like* felt easy, no big deal; probably because my feelings for them were no big deal. Easy.

But instinct told me Greg wouldn't be easy. As well, my feelings for Greg felt meaningful, messy, heady, intricate, and not entirely safe. He was not safe. Caution and sense told me that eventually these feelings would make me do something stupid, turn me into a fool, act against my best interests and better judgment.

Despite the warning bells, or maybe because they were so loud and persistent, I admitted the truth, "Yes, Greg. Yes, I feel it, too."

He said nothing else. I heard the suite door close after him, and I let my forehead fall to the door. There was no way I was going to be able to go back to sleep.

Part 3: There once was a ninja from Nantucket...

"YOU'RE A GYMNAST."

I flinched, my hands flew up, and gasped with startled fright at the owner of the voice.

"Sorry." Greg hovered at the entrance to the suite looking so handsome he made my chest hurt; I hadn't heard him come in.

I released a calming breath, my heart still thundering, and laughed at myself. "No, no. It's okay. I didn't hear you come in."

I saw he was wearing dark blue jeans that hung very nicely on his narrow hips and a long-sleeved grey thermal that made his eyes look almost black. Over his shoulder was a backpack. His dark hair was wet like he'd just showered, longish, yet achieved the effect of careless and wayward spikes. It needed a trim. I liked it.

"You're a gymnast," he repeated, edging further into the room.

I studied him, looking for some trace of a hangover or sign in his features that he was the same person who'd shown up the night before, knocking on my door and admitting he wanted to be my first everything.

But I didn't...or I couldn't. His gaze was back to its curious yet cautious state, the rest of his expression untroubled, calm.

"Yes, uh—well, no. I mean, I used to be a gymnast."

I wasn't calm. I couldn't seem to take a deep breath. Once again I felt the palpable current, a crackling awareness, and this time I knew it wasn't one-sided.

"How did you know?" My words were breathless, and I was staring at him, unable to look away.

"Fern told me. Can you still do a somersault?"

I nodded, no longer trusting my voice.

"A back flip?"

I nodded.

He examined me for a long stretch, giving nothing of his own thoughts away. Meanwhile, I burned under his dark gaze. His hands were stuffed in his pockets, and his attention moved over my body, marked with suspicion or something like it. I was still wearing my workout clothes because Dara and Hivan were in my dorm room solving world hunger.

Just kidding. They were having sex. Loudly.

I'd come back from a late afternoon trip to the gym to find my door closed and locked, Dara's suitcases piled up in the suite, and a sock on the doorknob.

I was waiting them out, rather than sneaking in, to grab some clothes.

Their sexcapades were gloriously awkward background music for my current conversation. I began to feel self-conscious of my yoga pants and sports bra in a way I'd never experienced before, wishing I'd left on my jacket.

Finally he said, "Prove it."

"Prove it?" I croaked.

"A back flip. I want to see a back flip."

I shook my head, holding his unreadable gaze, and feeling irritated by his complete lack of outward emotion, especially since I'd been waiting for him since early morning. When he hadn't shown by 4:30 p.m., I'd decided to burn off my frustration with a workout.

It was now past dinner time, and I was currently experiencing an uncomfortable and unfamiliar sense of discomposure. My body felt taut and primed; my heart was racing like I'd just finished a marathon.

He continued to look me over. His perusal affected me, heat spreading up my chest and spine. Then Greg claimed Dara's seat, setting his elbows on his long legs. He placed his backpack on the floor between his feet, and leaned toward me.

"Talk to me," he said.

"About gymnastics?"

"About anything."

I frowned at him; my heart hadn't yet evened, its pace still furious, frantic.

Clearing my throat and pressing my palm against the uncomfortable rhythm, I asked, "What do you want to know?"

He stared at me, then responded, "Everything."

"I'm not omniscient. I can't tell you everything."

This earned me a small smile, and his tone was softer when he asked, "Where did you grow up?"

"In Virginia, right outside of Washington, D.C."

He nodded like this made sense.

Then I asked, "How old are you?" before I quite knew what I was doing.

He answered without skipping a beat, "I'm twenty-three. What do your parents do? Where do they work?" He then pulled a bottle of tequila out of his backpack, along with two shot glasses, precut lemon wedges, and a small container of salt, and set the items on the desk. He arranged them with a neat efficiency that was distracting.

I eyeballed the liquor, though he made no attempt to pour. Instead, he leaned back in his chair, stretching his long, powerful legs in front of him, and rested one arm on the desk; his other large hand lay benignly on his thigh.

"My father is a vice president for one of the large defense contractors. My mother is a homemaker. What's a twenty-three-year-old doing living in a dorm?"

"I was in the Marines. I served for three years. On-campus housing is a lot less expensive than an apartment, and I like the atmosphere."

I couldn't tell if this last part was true or sarcasm; I was too distracted by the fact-bomb he'd just detonated, that he'd been in the Marines. He'd been in the Marines for three years.

"The...the U.S. Marines?"

"Yes. The United States Marines."

Greg seemed to sense that I needed a minute to absorb this information. He busied himself pouring two small shots of tequila and removing two lemon slices from the plastic bag before asking, "When did you stop doing gymnastics?"

"I was fourteen." I was too stunned to ask another question. I was thinking back to our last conversation in this suite area, when he'd told me that he'd fought for what he believed in, that it hadn't made any difference.

"Why did you stop?" he asked, reaching for my fingers where they rested on the open pages of my book.

I shook myself, recognized he was asking about gymnastics. "I got sick." His touch sent a shock up my arm; I gritted my teeth to keep from shivering.

"Sick? What kind of sick?" With no ceremony, Greg licked the back of my hand near my thumb sending a tremor of something both deliciously warm and delightfully cold through me. I gave into the shiver. He ignored it and sprinkled salt on the wet patch.

"I had a brain tumor." I hadn't meant to be so forthright, but my body was humming, ridiculously seized by the aftereffects of his tongue against my skin.

His hands stilled. In fact, everything about him stilled, and his eyes were affixed to my knuckles. His fingers tightened around mine.

"But you're okay now?"

I nodded even though he wasn't looking at my face. "Yes. I'm okay for now."

Greg's thumb stroked my index finger. He seemed to be meditating on it. His attention paired with Dara and Hivan's enthusiastic grunts and cries of pleasure were making me increasingly uncomfortable and aware of how very little clothing I was wearing.

My dissonance regarding having Greg here, alone with me, with two shots of tequila was growing. Especially since he'd *just* broken up with his girlfriend of over a year.

My attraction to him in that moment was heady, almost painful, just like I'd feared. I felt foolish.

"Greg," I withdrew my hand and placed it back on the open pages of my book. "Why are you here?"

"I broke up with Vanessa." His eyes met mine, and they matched his flat, matter-of-fact tone. He licked the skin adjacent to his thumb, holding my gaze.

"I know," I said on an exhale.

We stared at each other for a long moment.

He broke the silence, pouring salt on the back of his hand. "Aren't you going to ask why?"

I shook my head. "It's none of my business."

He didn't seem to like my answer because his mouth curved into a frown. Abruptly, Greg picked up a shot of tequila and handed it to me. I accepted it, glanced at the shot glass, then back at him. His attention made me feel like I was under a microscope.

"How old are you, Fiona?"

"I'm eighteen."

His eyes moved between mine. "Were you a good gymnast?"

"Yes. Very good."

"How good?"

"I placed second at the World Championships when I was thirteen and qualified for Team USA."

"Olympics?"

"Yes."

"And then you got sick."

"That's right."

"And how long were you sick?"

"Two and a half years."

"Chemotherapy?"

"No. Radiation."

"For two years?"

"Two and a half years."

Greg's jaw flexed; I saw the muscle at his temple jump before he said, "I'm a selfish bastard. You should know that about me."

I set the liquor down on the desk, tilted my head to the side, watching him. "What makes you think so?"

"Because I look at you, and I think, you and me, we're going to get married one day. And then, if you're a very good wife..." His eyes skated over my face as he paused, and it felt like a loving caress; but it also felt possessive and dangerous. His cadence dropped, deepened, as his stare settled on my lips. "If you're a very good wife, we'll have a mortgage."

I blinked. The lull of his voice masked the meaning of his words for a split second.

"A mortgage?"

He nodded. "Yes. And several children and perhaps a dog."

I'm sure I was looking at him like he was crazy, and I

followed my thoughts through with words, "You're crazy."

He nodded again. "I am."

"And abrupt and abrasive."

This earned me a pleased smile that stretched all the way to his eyes, making them warm and inviting. The effect left me breathless again.

"Yes. I'm also known for my inappropriate sense of humor, offensive jokes, and callous treatment of sensitive topics. I'm a sore loser and an even worse winner."

I shook my head at him, unable to help my smile. "Shouldn't you be playing up your good points? Isn't that what guys do when they're interested in a girl?"

"But you've never been kissed," he responded, his tone still flat but his eyes dancing with mischief, "and you've never dated. This is my chance to ruin you for anyone else."

"By telling me all about how terrible you are?"

"By being honest. By playing no games. When I tell you that I'm a selfish bastard, I mean it. And when I tell you that you're wonderful and amazing and stunning and definitely the most extraordinary woman I've ever met, you'll know I mean that, too."

My smile fell because I couldn't sustain it under the weight of his impassioned words, and my stupid heart thundered, galloped, beat out a violent staccato. I held perfectly still, watching him, suspicious of the feelings he'd stirred because they felt too big, irrational and uncontrollable.

I swallowed and managed to whisper, "You don't know me."

"Not all of you…" his eyes drifted to my lips and seemed to sharpen, "but I will."

"I have a date tomorrow, with Mark from art history," I

said dumbly. The words felt like a sad little shield against his onslaught of honesty.

"I know."

"I'm going."

"I know. You should."

I could barely breathe.

"You're confusing me," I said.

"You're a smart girl. You'll figure it out. And I...I will be patient."

Abruptly, I was aware that the suite had fallen silent; Dara and Hivan's activities had reached their natural conclusion. Comprehending this, I found I couldn't hold Greg's stare. My body felt needy, tight, straining, and restless. I didn't know what to do with myself.

All my life, my body had been a tool, frequently a disappointment, but not ever a part of me. First, because of the rigors of my training, it was a means to an end. Then during surgery and treatment, it felt like a failure.

But suddenly, in this room, with this man, it was my mind that felt disconnected from the rest of me. My body felt like it was the victim, on the side of right; my mind was the failure, the disappointment, the mess.

"However..."

Startled, I jumped when he spoke. I felt his hand reach out to remove the book from my lap. My eyes darted to his.

"... there is one thing I want, and I'm afraid time does not allow me to be patient on the matter."

Greg's eyes hijacked mine, his gaze intent and calculating. He stood, and tossed the book to the floor beside my chair. Looking down at me, he placed his knee between my legs and nudged them apart. I acquiesced without resistance.

He then placed his hands on me and spread my thighs, sending shocks of awareness to the pit of my stomach. My breath hitched as Greg knelt between my open legs and wrapped his big hands around my knees.

"I'm going to take this from you, but you shouldn't be surprised because you know I'm a selfish bastard." His voice was low, gravely, almost a whisper, his lips just inches from mine. "But I also want to make sure it's done right. I don't know this Mark from art history. He could be a rubbish kisser, scarring you for life. It might take me years of kiss-therapy to undo the damage."

Despite all the raging emotions and fluttering and twistings and hot flashes and yearning, his words struck me as hysterically funny. I pressed my lips together to keep from laughing.

His tone turned mock-stern, "Prepare yourself. I'm going to kiss you now."

I nodded once as I searched his eyes, finding them slightly hazy, dark and hot; and I knew—despite his protests to the contrary—his motives weren't entirely selfish. He'd guessed how I felt about him. He might be taking something, but he was also giving me a gift in return.

Greg paused, giving me a chance to push him away, though I sensed something like desperation behind his stare. I didn't push him away.

He closed his eyes.

I held my breath.

His generous mouth brushed mine.

A spike of something new and warm raced through me, making me tremble.

My eyelids drifted closed.

His fingers tightened on my legs.

I pressed my mouth to his.

He retreated a fraction, our lips separating, then returned, his head tilted slightly to the side, his mouth moving against mine, massaging.

I breathed him in, lifted my hands, and cupped his jaw, feeling like I needed to hold him in place.

He retreated again, again just a fraction, and returned to bite me lightly and lick my bottom lip.

I moaned.

His hands slid up my thighs, sending shivers straight to my lower belly.

I arched my back.

His grip settled on my waist, his palms on the bare skin of my midriff, his thumbs stroking my lower ribs.

I pressed my mouth more firmly to his, feeling a building sense of urgency.

But then, he retreated a third time, and this time he did not return.

I groaned.

He chuckled.

I opened one eye.

He was grinning.

I frowned. "No tongue?"

He laughed, obviously surprised, his smile brilliant, and cocked his head to the side as my hands moved to his shoulders.

"No guy should give you tongue for your first kiss. Tongue requires practice and feels like a slimy alien creature if you're not prepared for it, or if it's not done properly."

I laughed at his description. "So what do I need to do? How do I prepare for it?"

"Well…" his eyes unfocused as they moved to some

spot behind me, and his voice adopted an instructional air. "First you have to want it-"

"I want it."

His smile was quick and just as quickly suppressed. He cleared his throat. "Well, then, I shall give it to you."

I closed my eyes immediately and lifted my chin in offering, expecting him to lean forward as he'd done before, feeling giddy and excited and a bit intoxicated. I waited, my hands on his shoulders, his on my stomach.

When he didn't come to me, my lashes fluttered open. I found Greg watching me, his brown eyes looking lost, almost mournful, as they moved over my face.

"Ask me when I knew," he said.

I frowned, confused by his request, and studied him, hoping I'd discover his meaning. At length, still perplexed, I did as he instructed.

"When did you know?"

I watched him take a breath, and with it all pretense fell away. All his walls, all his cleverness, all his grandstanding and pretending. He looked vulnerable, and it made my chest ache.

"When I saw you…" he whispered, leaning forward, his eyes on mine, until he became blurry. He slid his nose against my nose, nipped my bottom lip. My mouth parted in response.

"I saw you…" he kissed my parted lips, "you'd bent over to pick up your pen, or some such item…" he kissed me again, this time on the corner of my mouth, and my eyelids fell, my heart swelling, my breath catching, "and I thought to myself…" one more press of his lips on my jaw, "I thought, I am going to tap that ass."

My eyes flew open, as did my mouth, and my head reared back, "Greg!"

"And other things!" He grinned, wagging his eyebrows,

pulling me forward, "I thought, *I am going to tap that ass,* as well as other things, all having to do with how lovely you are and how much I respect you as a person."

Uncontainable laughter erupted from my chest, and I pushed him away, "You're unbelievable!"

"Yes, darling." He kissed my neck as I leaned away. "I hear that all the time."

I barked another laugh and shook my head, his kisses hot against my neck, sending tremors of delight racing through me. "Get off of me!"

"I will, but first I must taste you..." He bit my neck, making me moan.

He did this for a while, kneeling before me, his hands roaming, my limbs growing limp, and heat gathering in my stomach. Eventually his mouth found its way back to mine, and he kissed me, this time with tongue.

He was right.

It did feel like a slimy alien creature—for about three seconds.

Then it felt wonderful.

Part 4: Did you hear about the ninja who invented knock-knock jokes?

I HAD A NICE time on my Valentine's Day date with Mark from art history.

I did.

I really did.

No, really. I did.

He was… nice. He had polite table manners. He didn't argue when I insisted we split the check. And when the conversation ebbed, I would ask him a question about class or feign ignorance of nineteenth century impressionists.

I felt guilty about the periods of stunted conversation because they were usually my fault. Mark would be talking and my mind would wander to Greg. I'd wonder what he was doing. I'd wonder why he didn't object when I insisted that I go on this date with Mark. I'd wonder whether he'd decided to spend Valentine's Day with someone else…

And then my heart hurt, and my throat would become suddenly dry and I would be slightly nauseous, and the conversation would stall, and I would feel bad.

Aside from my fixation on another man, the date was nice.

Well, it was nice right up until the point where we were ten snowy steps from my dorm and I was just about to thank him for the very nice evening. He blindsided me by affixing his lips to mine, assaulting my mouth with his tongue. I was unprepared and didn't immediately respond. Apparently, he was also unprepared because we just stood there unmoving, his hands gripping my arms, his lips pressed to mine, and his tiny tongue impaling my lips, like he was only giving me the tip.

It was stiff and straight. He didn't move or relax it, and given my lack of experience I wasn't sure what to do. Honestly, I was afraid to touch it with my tongue or suck on it, like I'd done with Greg, because Mark might interpret that as permission to take up residence in my mouth for a longer period of time with his small, stabby tongue.

I just wanted this imposter of a kiss to be over.

I started counting in my head, figuring when I got to ten I would gently push him away, thank him for a very nice date, and rush into my building.

That is not what happened.

When I reached number four, I heard a throat clear.

Then I heard a familiar masculine voice with a familiar posh British accent drawl, "I do wonder, are you quite well?"

Mark stiffened further—which I hadn't thought possible—and pushed me away slightly, releasing my upper arms and turning wide eyes in the direction of the interrupting voice.

"I... uh, what?"

"I said, are you well? I was worried you'd gotten stuck like that. Oh, I do hope I didn't interrupt an experiment of some sort."

Greg was leaning against one of the double doors of our

dorm, propping it open, and… smoldering. I was half surprised he didn't melt the snow around his feet.

And I felt it.

The attraction, the pull.

This feeling between us—of expectation and excitement—wasn't something I knew how to compartmentalize. When I'd thought it was one-sided, it had been easier to control, explain away as an unrequited crush. But now I knew he felt it too. I wanted to be with him all the time. Concentrating on anything other than him was almost impossible.

His hair was ruffled, askew, like he'd been asleep or he'd run his fingers through it several times. He was dressed in dark jeans, boots, and an olive green long-sleeved T-shirt that highlighted his long, narrow torso. His arms were crossed over his chest, and his expression was all solicitous and concerned curiosity as he peered at Mark.

And yet, behind the polite façade I sensed something lurking. Something not concerned or solicitous. Something impolite.

Despite the pull of my attraction to him and the way my body instantly responded to his voice and mere presence, Greg wasn't the only one feeling impolite. Throwing a glare in Greg's direction—hoping it disguised the extent to which he flustered me by existing—I turned my attention back to Mark just as he spoke.

"Um, I- no. We're not experimenting. I'm kissing my date goodnight here, man. Could you give us a minute?" Mark's eyes flickered to mine, his pale cheeks flushing pink; the color contrasted with his wheat complexion. He took a step away from me. "I'm sorry."

I tilted my head to the side and gave him a reassuring smile. I was about to yield to my instincts and ease his discomfort, when Greg called to us again.

"Kissing? Is that what you call that?" He whistled low then added, "If that's how you kiss then you *should* apologize."

I tried not to grimace. I tried, and failed.

Mark's attention moved from me to Greg, then back again. "Who is this guy?"

I sighed, my flustered frustration punctuated by the puff of white condensation as I exhaled. "That's Greg."

"Greg?"

"Yes. Greg. He… lives on my floor."

Mark's eyes narrowed.

"Is he your boyfriend?"

"No," I said.

"Not yet," Greg added helpfully.

My grimace morphed into a scowl and my betraying heart quadrupled with traitorous glee as I sought to clarify, "Greg lives on my floor. He's not my boyfriend. I wouldn't have gone on a date with you if I had a boyfriend."

Why I felt the need to clarify wasn't exactly clear since I had no intention of going out with Mark again; yet the thought of Mark walking away from this evening thinking of me as a bad person didn't sit right either.

Mark's expression softened just before Greg

volunteered, "That's right. We're not dating. We just make out sometimes, like yesterday."

I couldn't help it, I groaned. And it wasn't just a grown of embarrassment, but a semi-moan of remembering what it was like to make out with Greg. Making out with Greg was beyond divine and he certainly never rationed his tongue.

Out of nowhere, I was having a hot flash.

I closed my eyes and let my chin drop to my chest, painful mortification expanding like an inflating balloon from the pit of my stomach to the back of my throat. Strangely, I didn't feel embarrassed for myself; rather, I felt terribly sorry for Mark and regretful of the situation.

And I felt like a bad person.

I heard Mark's boots crunch on the snow as he backed away from me, his voice ripe with disdain. "I thought you were a nice girl, Fiona. I guess I was wrong. You don't have to worry about me calling you again, that's for certain."

Cringing, bracing for what I felt sure I would find, I lifted my gaze and found Mark staring at me with resolute indictment.

When our eyes met, he warned hatefully, "And don't come to me for help when you can't tell Manet from Monet."

With that he huffed, turned, and stomped off. I watched him go until he moved beyond the perimeter of the dorm lights and was swallowed by the dark Valentine's night.

Mark really was a nice guy. It really had been a nice date. Just nice. Not great, not fun, not interesting or thrilling or exciting. Just... nice.

And very, very wrong.

Maybe Mark was right. Maybe I wasn't nice. Maybe my feelings of self-reproach and guilt were warranted. Maybe I shouldn't have gone on a date with Mark when I was more than interested in—and by interested in I mean utterly infatuated with—Greg.

This was messy.

I heard Greg clear his throat again, rather obnoxiously, pulling me from my thoughts. I gathered a steadying breath and affixed Greg with a suspicious glare, hoping it communicated the weight of my ire.

"I'm not talking to you," I said through gritted teeth. I was mad of course, but mostly at myself.

"I see. You're struck speechless with gratitude. Don't fret too much," he gave me a half smile as his gaze swept up, then down my body, adding darkly, "I'm not all that interested in talking anyway."

I made a sound in the back of my throat that I wasn't expecting, a half swallow-misfire half huff, and turned completely around to face him. And, confound it, I was blushing.

He was beyond exasperating. Just yesterday he'd encouraged me to go on the date with Mark. In fact, after he gave me my first kiss and first French kiss, he'd *insisted* I go on the date with Mark. Then he packed up his tequila and left. Then he'd avoided me all day. So why was he now standing there behaving like the jealous boyfriend?

I leveled him with what I hoped was an incendiary stare

as I stomped past him into the dorm, and made a beeline for the stairwell.

He was close behind me. At first I felt his nearness, then as we ascended the stairs I heard the resonance of his footsteps in rhythm with mine.

We climbed two flights, the atmosphere between us crackling with tension, each step a chapter of unsaid words. My accelerated heartbeat had very little to do with the stairs I was taking two at a time. I kept expecting him to touch me, stop me, ask me to listen to some explanation for his behavior.

But he didn't.

Unable to endure another second of this silent torture, I spun abruptly and pointed my finger at his face, demanding, "Why did you do that?"

If he was surprised by my questioning, he didn't look it. To my complete exasperation, he appeared entirely unfazed.

"Why did I do what?" He shrugged.

"Why did you interrupt my date with Mark?"

"I'll give you three guesses." His voice was steady, but his mouth curved into a derisive twist, and his eyes narrowed.

I studied him, his achingly handsome face and his dark eyes glaring at mine with mocking accusation. "Greg, you insisted that I go! You could have asked me not to go."

His left eyebrow hitched and I wasn't surprised when his words arrived deadpan and sarcastic. "What? After he'd already made the reservations for Applebees'? That would have been extraordinarily poor form. That is where he took you on your *Valentine's* date, isn't it? Applebee's?"

"No," I groused, then rolled my eyes, admitting, "He took me to Olive Garden."

Greg made a clicking sound with his tongue and walked around me to the next flight of stairs, mumbling, "Of course he did."

Now I was climbing after him. "There is nothing wrong with Applebee's or Olive Garden and you didn't answer my question. If you didn't want me to go, why didn't you say something? Why encourage me to go on a date with another man if you didn't want me to go?"

Greg's laugh was loud and sharp and sudden. "Fiona, you didn't go on a date with a man. If Mark from art history had been a man I would have sabotaged the evening early on. As it was, you went on a date with a nineteen-year-old boy. I didn't need to raise a finger. Nineteen-year-old boys are harmless."

"And when you were nineteen you were harmless?" My voice echoed in the cavernous stairwell.

He stopped suddenly and turned. His jaw was set and his usually generous lips were pressed together in a firm, angry line. Greg backed me up against the stair railing and peered down at me with heavy-lidded eyes shadowed by thick black lashes.

When he answered I felt the heat from his body, scant inches separating us; his words were low and dark, just a rumble above a whisper. "You know better, Darling. I've never been harmless. And it's a good thing too, because you don't want harmless."

I succeeded in maintaining eye contact—I even managed

a stubborn chin tilt—and was able to toss back, "You might be right, maybe harmless doesn't appeal to me much. But this feels a lot like playing games, Greg. And playing games doesn't appeal to me either."

His eyes darted between mine. I could tell I'd surprised him because his angry expression was eclipsed by thoughtful deliberation. He appeared to be struggling.

At last, with measured sounding gentleness, he asked, "What appeals to you, Fiona?"

"Honesty. Sincerity." Then, because I'd just told him to be honest and I didn't want to be a coward or a hypocrite, I added weakly, "You."

Greg visibly relaxed, the tight line of his lips smoothing. "When I'm being honest?"

"Yes."

He continued to scrutinize me as he gathered a deep breath, and in doing so his chest brushed against mine. I felt debilitated by his nearness. Seconds ticked by. He said nothing.

If I'd known him better I might've been able to decipher the puzzle of his expression. It occurred to me that the feeling between us, this intangible magnetic field of mutual esteem, might be fleeting. Perhaps it was premature, and based on presumption rather than reality. He was so handsome, so charming, so uniquely charismatic. But what did I really *know* about him?

Before I could travel too far down the road of doubt, he said, "I'm going to start calling you Fe."

"Why? A nickname for Fiona?"

"No. Because you have nerves of steel. I'm not typically

a game player. When I'm around you…" He stopped, swallowed, his dark eyes a little desperate. "I was going to say, *you make me crazy*. But it's not you, it's me. I make me crazy, thinking about you. Does that make sense?"

I nodded, feeling myself thaw.

He continued haltingly, "I *did* want you to go on this date with Creepy Mark from art history."

"He's not creepy-"

"He is creepy. He looks like one of the children of the corn, and take into account that we're currently in Iowa where corn fields abound. He may have been attempting to suck the soul out of your body down there, because that definitely wasn't kissing."

I found myself trying not to laugh. "Greg-"

"But you…" He pressed his lips together again, his eyebrows pulling into a tight, unhappy line. "After you left, the thought of you out with someone else, I didn't like it. And I don't want you to do it again."

"I can't not go out with anyone else ever again. That's crazy. I have study groups and class projects." I kept my tone even, reasonable.

"I'll overlook your atrocious double negative for now, because that's not what I meant." He took a step back and reached for my hand, cradling it between his large palms and shifting his focus to where we touched. "I wanted you to go out on a date with Creepy Mark because I was certain it would be a disappointment. But when you left, it didn't matter if you had a good time or not. It was a date, a romantic situation if you will. Certainly you'll have study groups and class projects in the future. But I want to be your only source of romantic situations from this point forward."

I felt my mouth pull to one side as I watched him speak, because Greg Archer was completely adorable when he was honest and sincere.

I squeezed his hand and reclaimed the step toward him, drawing his eyes back to mine. "I would like the reverse to be true as well. I would like to be your only source of romantic situations from this point forward."

He sighed, it sounded both happy and forlorn. "Even if you didn't want it, it's yours. It's been just twenty-four hours and I'm ruined."

"You're ruined?" I grinned.

"Yes. I've been through all my best pornography videos this evening and nothing interests me."

My mouth fell open.

"If you want to know the truth, I'm rather upset about it. I've invested quite a lot of money in the *Debbie Does* series, and now it's all rubbish."

I pulled my hand out of his, prepared to be outraged, but instead I laughed. "You're appalling."

His eyes twinkled with mischief, but his face and tone remained serious. "It's pronounced *appealing,* Darling. And I don't suppose I could talk you into recording some videos? My birthday is in September."

I shook my head and walked around him to the last flight of stairs. "I'm not talking to you about your porn addiction."

"I'm not addicted to porn, but I was very fond of it. It's helped me through some difficult times and answered so many important questions from my youth, for example—pizza delivery women, as a subset of society, are sexually adventurous and are apparently paid well enough that they can afford breast implants. Did you know that?"

He sounded so epically sincere, I couldn't stop laughing.

"And babysitters across this great country suffer from a very peculiar type of alopecia."

"What?"

"They're hairless, in their *lady closet.*"

"Ah! Stop!" I'm sure my cheeks were bright red.

He had to pull me up the last few steps because he wouldn't stop regaling me with universal truths revealed to him via porn—all of which were horribly hilarious nonsense. By the time we reached my suite my jaw hurt and I was wiping at my eyes.

"Your jokes are terrible."

Greg grinned, walking me backwards into my suite and wagging his eyebrows he corrected me, "It's pronounced *tremendous.*"

***

I LOOKED UP from my textbook as my headphones were pulled from my ears. Fern was standing in front of me, bent at the waist. Her face inches from my face. She was smiling.

"You and Greg," she said.

I blinked at her. "Uh…"

"You. And. Greg." She placed my headphones on the desk and straightened, her eyes big and round. I hadn't seen her since the Thursday before Valentine's Day.

"Me and Greg?"

"You're together." She paired this statement with an emphatic hand wave.

I gathered a large breath—stalling, trying to read her mood—then released it slowly. "Yes. I mean, I guess so."

"You *guess* so? You don't know so?"

If being each other's only source of romantic situations from now meant that we were officially together, then we were officially together.

I straightened in my seat and replied with conviction, "No. You're right. We're together. I know so."

After our stairway conversation, I'd invited Greg into my room because I wanted him there, not because I had any designs or plans in mind. He'd suggested we stay in the suite instead, placing me between his legs on the floor and rubbing my back. We talked until late, past 2:00 A.M., and munched on snacks of apples and string cheese. He bid me goodnight with a gentle, lingering kiss, and promises to return the next afternoon.

It was now the next afternoon.

Fern pressed her lips together. Her gaze moved over me and I suspected she was debating her next words. I was mildly alarmed because I'd never known Fern to be circumspect.

"What's wrong?" I finally asked.

"Someone saw the two of you last night in the hallway, and then Greg leaving late at night."

I frowned. Why anyone would care enough to tell Fern? And if they'd told Fern, how many other people knew? And what difference did it make? And why was it anyone else's business?

"Girls like Greg," she said with a loud suddenness, like it was a warning.

Ah... okay. Now I get it.

I widened my eyes and closed my book. "I see."

Fern huffed dramatically then fell into the chair next to mine. "What I mean is, Greg *just* broke up with Vanessa, and now the two of you are together. This dorm can be worse than high school. We're basically trapped in these walls until the snow melts, and small minds are occupied with the affairs of other people, especially when one of those people is Greg Archer."

I squirmed uncomfortably and set my book aside. "I didn't make a play for him, if that's what people are saying."

"I know. You're not like that."

"I didn't go to high school, Fern. And I've watched more TV over the last four months than I was allowed to watch during my entire childhood. I'm not used to my personal life being of interest to anyone." Mostly because I'd never had a personal life.

"You were sheltered, I know." She gave me a sympathetic smile.

"I'm not completely ignorant."

"I know."

"I understand the dynamics of competition."

"But you're used to defined rules for competition. *All is fair in love and war.*"

I grimaced. "What should I do?"

"Nothing. Just be you. But don't be surprised if some of the girls are-"

"Unfriendly?"

"Maybe. Maybe even friendlier than before. They'll just be bitchy about it. Prepare yourself for lots of questions and judgment. Trust no one."

Suddenly, I had heartburn. "That sounds lonely."

She shrugged. "Girls are mean."

"Not all girls."

"No, not all girls." She gave me a resigned smile and added, "Just most girls."

A knock on the door to our suite interrupted our conversation.

"Who is it?" Fern called, giving me a bracing look.

"Pizza," came a muffled male reply.

Fern and I exchanged questioning glances as she stood. "What? Pizza?"

"Mail," another muffled response, followed quickly by, "Candygram."

Comprehension claimed her features and she pressed her lips together, trying not to smile, and called back, "Go away. We want no land sharks here."

Confused, I mouthed the words *land sharks?* at her.

She rolled her eyes, "It's from Saturday Night Live. There's this shark at the door to the Weekend Update desk, and he…" she tossed her hands in the air and moved to the door. I heard her unlock it; I hadn't realized it was locked. "Never mind. I'll just get my hands on some old episodes."

She pulled the suite door open and stepped back, motioning for whoever it was to enter. "Enter. She's all yours."

Greg sauntered into the room, grinning at Fern and looking delectable. "Thanks, Fern. You're a pal."

I sat straighter, a spike of awareness passing through me like a shock, arresting my breath for a span of five seconds and tightening my throat. His eyes moved to me and his grin wavered. We watched each other for... I honestly don't know how long.

"*Riiiight*," Fern's elongated word pulled me out of my stupor, "I'm going to *go* so you two can have uninterrupted eye-sex."

Greg and I spoke over each other.

"You don't have to leave," I said.

"Don't let me keep you," he said.

Fern rolled her eyes again and chuckled.

I gave Greg a disapproving frown. "Where will you go? It's supposed to snow all day."

"I'll be back before it gets dark," she said, waving away my concern and grabbing her bag. "We're supposed to get ten inches overnight."

Greg opened the door for Fern and mumbled under his breath, "I might give Fiona ten inches this afternoon, if she plays her cards right."

Um... hello!

Both Fern and I gaped at him, wearing mirrored expressions of shock, and the suite plunged into dead quiet for a protracted moment. But then Fern threw her head back and burst out laughing. Greg's shoulders also shook with silent laughter, giving me a look that was both apologetic and unrepentant.

I didn't laugh. I lowered my eyes to the brown carpet and proceeded to turn bright red. My cheeks were flaming because:

Naked Greg.

Naked me.

Bed.

Floor.

Desk.

Mouth.

Hands.

Hot breath.

Ten inches.

I was… overwhelmed with visual imagery. The charged atmosphere between us persisted. Visual imagery plus charged atmosphere made me hot. Which made me embarrassed and unsteady. Which made me turn red.

I forced myself to smile, but it was weak; I needed a minute. "Let me go grab some snacks, I'll be right back."

I knew his eyes were on me because I could feel the weight of them as I left. I paced to my mini fridge and opened it, grabbed a can of Coke and pressed it to my neck, telling myself I was ridiculous. It was a joke, just a joke. I may have been inexperienced but I wasn't a prude.

I was… caught unawares, I reasoned. *I'll be ready next time. I'll be bold.*

I knew when Fern departed because I heard their

murmured conversation come to an end, punctuated by the closing of the suite door. I put the Coke back on the shelf and inspected the fridge, distracting myself with its contents and hoping the cold air would help cool me down.

My back was to the entrance of the room and I was absorbed in *not* thinking about Greg's alleged ten inches, so I started when I heard the door to my room close. I turned my head and found Greg leaning against it, looking at me.

I gave him a tight smile. "Are you hungry?"

He paused, like a witty retort was on the tip of his tongue, but must've thought better of it because he shook his head, saying nothing.

The charged atmosphere grew tenfold, was positively electric.

I managed to swallow and straighten from the fridge, closing it as I stood and saying honestly, "It's good to see you."

His answering genuine smile made my heart thunder. Why was I so nervous? I told myself to calm down.

Greg stepped away from the door. He made a small circle, glancing around the room and paying special attention to my half. At length he declared, "So this is your room."

"Yes. This is my room."

He gestured to the walls. "You have no posters up."

"Correct." I was happy to be discussing a topic as benign as posters.

Greg surveyed me. "Why don't you have any posters?"

"I guess I haven't found any that I want to look at every day." My attention flickered to Dara's side, to her ten or more posters and pictures wallpapering the plain white paint. I hadn't noticed how bare my side looked in comparison.

"Interesting. What's this?" He picked up the book on my nightstand, a practical pictorial guide to mixed martial arts, and flipped through it. "Are you interested in martial arts?"

"Yes."

"Are you going to beat me up?" He gave me a sideways glance.

"Not unless you give me a reason." I crossed to him and took the book out of his hands, setting it back on the table. "Are you going to go through all my things?"

"Yes, starting with your panty drawer. Be a good girl and point me in the right direction."

I forced a chuckle, reminding myself to be bold, and sat on my bed. "Go ahead, snoop. I have nothing to hide."

His gaze skittered over me, considering. After a short pause, he stepped forward and sat next to me. My heart jumped to my throat and I tensed in anticipation. We were alone together, in my dorm room. The door was closed. Anything could happen.

How wonderfully exciting.

Greg bounced a few times, flattening his hands over the mattress as though testing the springs. "I think your bed is firmer than mine. And it squeaks less."

"You should file a complaint." My tone was tighter than I wanted so I tried to swallow… and failed. I took a deep, calming breath.

"I should. Or," he lifted his eyebrows meaningfully, "I could just steal yours."

"Or…" I cleared my throat to dispel the nervousness, placed my hands on his chest, and gently pushed him down on the mattress. I finished my thought as I settled next to him, "You could sleep in here with me."

I was being bold and brave and not a prude. But I'm sure the effect of seductress was ruined by my shaking hands and voice. I tried not to wince at the terse awkwardness of my attempt. I was bad at this.

Greg cocked an eyebrow, narrowing his eyes. Again he looked like he was biting back a retort, literally this time— he was biting his bottom lip—his gaze assessing.

At length, he gathered a deep breath and said, "You look like one of those sorts who has perpetually cold feet and stabby toenails." As though to illustrate his point, his foot played with mine at the end of the bed. "But I do enjoy your hermit socks. Where can I get a pair of these?"

I realized he was trying to disarm his earlier sexual innuendo, encourage me to relax with benign teasing. I was grateful, but it also made me feel naïve and inadequate.

But then again, I was naïve. I was unworldly, and I couldn't become worldly overnight.

"I knit these hermit socks." I poked his foot with mine and grinned when I realized we were playing footsie.

"You knit those socks?" He sounded impressed. "Do all hermits knit?"

"Yes." I nodded. "Especially misogynistic manifesto

writing hermits."

He lifted his head, inspecting our feet as they continued to play, then leaned his head toward mine. "These socks scream, *Ask me about my thirteen cats!*" Greg whispered, his eyes widening for a beat, his mouth forming a crooked grin.

I smiled at him as I giggled, reaching forward and enjoying the connection, the warm solidness of his stomach and chest under my fingertips. We were laying on our sides, face-to-face, so close I was able to count his freckles. The light from the window behind me highlighted the flecks of gold and copper in his dark irises. I was lost to the moment, fuzzy headed with possibility, allowing myself to be caught in the halo of his strength and... maleness.

Then he said, "You're beautiful."

I blinked his face back into focus, feeling flush with pleasure, and unable to contain my smile. "Thank you."

He wasn't smiling; his gaze sharpened, the curve of his mouth almost stern. "I don't know that you understand my meaning. Allow me to explain."

I nodded, still smiling despite his somberness. I couldn't help it. The boy... rather, the *man* I couldn't stop thinking about had just told me I was beautiful. I wasn't coming down from the clouds anytime soon.

"Do you know who Henry Rollins is?"

"The singer?"

He bobbed his head back a forth in a small considering movement. "Technically he's a spoken word artist, but what he is or isn't doesn't relate to my point. Sometimes his words are nonsense, rubbish, innocuous propaganda. And sometimes his words are..." Greg paused, drawing his bottom lip into his mouth and staring through me. He was quiet, obviously debating how to adequately describe what Henry Rollins' words sometimes are.

Suddenly he quoted, "'*Girls aren't beautiful, they're pretty. Beautiful is too heavy a word to assign to a girl. Women are beautiful because their faces show that they know they have lost something... and gained something else.'"*

My smile faded as we stared at each other, the full meaning and implication of Greg's use of the word *beautiful* registering in increments. His eyes warmed, and I realized his hand was resting on my hip, his fingertips slipping under the hem of my shirt. I shivered involuntarily at the contact.

When he spoke next his voice was a whisper, like he was sharing a secret. "I've often wondered why you are so beautiful when everyone else is merely pretty."

I lifted my hand to his cheek, molded my palm against his strong jaw. "What do you think I've lost, Greg?"

He covered my hand with his and I mourned the loss of his light touches on my back. "Vanity."

"Vanity?" His answer surprised and confused me.

"Yes. An aggrandized lack of self-awareness, a yearning to be coveted as the center of the universe. You've lost the desire for a self-centered manifest destiny."

"And here I thought you were referring to my hair loss." I tried to lighten the mood.

"No you didn't," he challenged, narrowing his eyes.

Then apropos of nothing, he asked, "What was your childhood like?"

I shifted an inch away, my hand falling to the bed between us. "Um, fine."

"Not happy. Not terrible. Just fine?"

"Yeah."

"Define *fine*."

I debated how to answer this question because I had very few positive feelings about my childhood. My mother was an irrational screamer who required constant management and handling. My father was hardly around due to his job, but I'm sure he loved me in his own way. I'd started college ignorant of the world. I would never have a fulfilling relationship with either of my parents.

Yet making complaints about my privileged upbringing struck me as petulant and entitled.

"I had a roof, clothes, food, safety. I have a younger sister I adore. I have parents who... do their best."

Greg's grin returned and I was happy to see it. "See? No vanity. You've lost the ability to care about bullshit that doesn't matter. You're a star, the center of a solar system, with no desire for the planets, asteroids, and moons caught in your gravitational field."

"Who wants creepy planets anyway? Planets are amoebas, circling mindlessly in the vacuum of space. They're star stalkers of the worst sort."

He continued to look at me like I was a treasure. "Planets are creepy, when you put it like that."

I looped a finger into his jeans pocket and tugged lightly. "What about you? What was your childhood like?"

His grin turned brittle and his attention moved to the right, beyond my head to the window behind me. "My parents' house was in Mayfair, but I went to boarding school. My father was a banker and my mother was the daughter of an earl."

Whoa...!

Mayfair— an exclusive area of West London, by the east edge of Hyde Park, in the City of Westminster—was one of the most expensive postal codes in the world, home of aristocrats and billionaires.

"An earl? Your grandfather is an-"

He spoke over me, giving me the sense that he needed to finish now that he'd started. "My father killed himself when I was fifteen. Apparently he was terribly corrupt, stole millions of dollars from people, very bad man. I have few memories of him, and none of them pleasant. My mother died the year after, an overdose. I was sent to live with my father's half-sister in California when I was sixteen."

"Oh my God." I released the words on an exhale, unable to mask my astonished dismay and empathy. Reaching forward, I wrapped my arms around his neck, holding him tightly, as though I could hug away his past hurts and disappointments.

After a moment, his arms came around me as well. He buried his head in my neck, therefore his words were muffled as he continued, "She lived in Compton, just outside of Los Angeles."

I jerked my head back and stared at him, my mouth gaping. "Your aunt lived in *Compton*? *The* Compton?

Like, the home of Dr. Dre and Easy-E?"

"The one and only."

"You moved to Compton when you were sixteen? After living in Mayfair?"

"It was a very different environment, and yet also extremely similar. Did you know they have a cricket team?"

"The city of Compton has a cricket team?"

"Oh yes. It's called the Compton Cricket Club, founded a few years ago at the Dome Village Homeless Community in L.A. I was one of the charter members when I was in high school. *Gangsta, Gangsta* by N.W.A. was our victory song."

A disbelieving laugh tumbled from my lips. My Greg was a walking, talking contradiction.

"Another similarity, I'd come home after high school and frequently find random crackheads milling about outside, offering to prostitute themselves for a few dollars. Once or twice I found one in my room, going through my belongings, looking for something of value to steal."

"How is that similar to living in Mayfair?"

"My mother's friends often milled about, prostituting themselves for scraps of attention. And I used to find my mother—who was addicted to any number of prescription medications—going through my belongings when my father would cut her off, looking for something of value to steal." He chuckled as he finished drawing the comparison, like his past was hilariously ironic rather than heartbreakingly tragic.

"Oh Greg…" I couldn't laugh with him, so I kissed him.

Soft, slow kisses, first on the lips, then on his forehead, temple, and jaw. His hand slipped beneath my shirt, gripping my bare back and holding me steady.

I heard him sigh, like a contented cat. And I thought I also heard him purr—not actually purr, more like a rumbly, pleased groan—before we were interrupted by a door slamming and raised voices in the suite area. I stiffened, reluctantly glancing up from Greg's lovely neck.

I didn't want to retreat. He smelled like hints of warm skin, oranges, and spicy aftershave, the good kind that makes the chest feel airy and light. But based on the volume of their drama, Dara and Hivan were only moments away from bursting into the room and kicking us out.

I pulled my hand through my hair and gave Greg an apologetic look. "I guess we should get going."

"Why?"

"That's Dara and Hivan."

I moved to sit and he stopped me. "So?"

"So, they're going to want to come in here to fight."

"…so?" He paired this with a single eyebrow lift.

"So, we should leave."

"Why should we leave? Don't they do this all the time?"

"Well, yes. About once a week."

Greg snorted, his arm tightening around my waist. "Then they should leave. We were here first."

"But…" I faltered, because the reason was obvious. "They need privacy."

Hivan's bellowing greeted our ears, causing Greg to roll

his eyes. "They don't want privacy. They want an audience. A pair of pribbling base-court varlots."

"Pribbling base-court varlots? What does that even mean?"

"It's a Shakespearean insult. Roughly translated, it means selfish twats."

I gave him a squinty grin despite Dara and Hivan's shouting match outside the door.

Greg's eyes flickered to my mouth and his tugged in response. "I'm not ready to leave yet."

"We'll go to the library," I suggested, not wanting to leave either, but recognizing the futility of the desire.

"No. Hang the library. I want to stay here with you." Abruptly, he rolled to the edge of the bed and stood. With his hands on his hips he glowered at all four corners of my room.

"What are you looking for?" I rose to a sitting position.

"Where are your tissues?"

"There." I pointed to a wire shelf at the end of my bed.

He pulled three tissues from the box and handed them to me. "Pretend like you're crying."

"What?" I accepted the tissues and swung my feet to the floor.

"Just, do it. When they come in, pretend like you're crying." He flicked his hand impatiently.

"Greg-"

He cut me off, shouting, "O serpent heart hid with a flowering face!" Then bent toward me and said in a rushed whisper, "Follow my lead."

I stared at him askance, his words both odd and strangely familiar. I wasn't sure if I wanted to reject this silliness or play along. But I had no time to ponder, because Dara opened the door. Her back was to us and Hivan was yelling at her.

I only caught the tail end of his rant, "... such bullshit, Dara! I was with you the entire time, you always see things that aren't there. Stop being so fucking paranoid."

"You were not with me the whole time. I saw you! You were all over her, Hivan! Don't pretend like it didn't happen. I am so done with you! I hate you!" Her screeching, tearful response reminded me to bring the tissue to my nose.

Greg pulled his hands through his hair and shouted— with feeling—over the last part of Dara's accusation, "Did ever a dragon keep so fair a cave? Beautiful tyrant! Fiend angelical! Dove feather raven, wolvish-ravening lamb!"

My eyes bulged because I realized what he was doing. I didn't recognize the play, but I was almost certain he was quoting Shakespeare.

Hivan shifted uncomfortably, taking one step inside the room, "Uh... guys, could we have some privacy-"

Greg cut him off and stabbed an accusing finger at me. "Despised substance of devinest show, just opposite to what thou justly seemest - A dammed saint, an honorable villain! Hmm? Speak! Or hadst thou to do in hell when thou didst bower the spirit of a fiend in moral paradise of such sweet flesh?"

My shoulders started to shake with silent laughter and I had to cover the lower half of my face with the tissue as I stared at him. He gnashed his teeth, threw his arms around with exaggerated movements. I shook my head at his ridiculous raging, which sounded oddly appropriate in his accent. He ignored me, seemingly lost to the scene he was reciting.

"Was ever book containing such vile matter so fairly bound? Oh no! No! I canst not stand it!" Greg ceased stomping around the room turned toward the open door, as though just noticing we had company. Both Dara and Hivan's eyes widened and, in unison, the couple took a step back. Greg charged toward them, chasing them out of the room while continuing to shout-recite, "Oh, that deceit should dwell in such a gorgeous palace. Shame. Shame on thee!"

And with that, he slammed the door in both their faces.

Part 5: Why did the ninja cross the road?

GREG WANTED ME to do a backflip.

He didn't pester me about it, not at all. But he did mention it on more than one occasion.

I agreed, since it was simple enough, on the condition he would be the only person to see it. I didn't want anyone else to watch. My abilities felt personal to me now, and I didn't like the idea of sharing that part of myself with strangers—not anymore. But the ground outside was frozen. We were surrounded by several feet of snow. The only space big enough and warm enough for any acrobatics was the lobby of the dorm.

During the second week of March a plan was devised. We decided to meet in the lobby at 3:00 a.m., and I would show him a backflip.

That day we met after classes, grabbed dinner at the café on campus, tried to study but ended up debating the merits of Hong Kong returning to Chinese rule, then parted ways around 11:30 p.m. My alarm clock went off at 2:50 a.m., giving me just enough time to rub the sleep from my eyes, brush my teeth at my desk, and pull on a sweatshirt. I wasn't terribly surprised to find Greg standing outside the door to my suite. But I was impressed when he handed me a mug of hot coffee.

"I don't know what a xenophobic hermit requires in the morning, so I made coffee." His voice was hushed.

"Coffee works," I whispered and took a sip of the black liquid, found it magnificently strong, "as long as it was made with the tears of women and children."

Greg flashed me a grin that made my stomach do backflips. "Is there any other way to make coffee?"

I hid my smile with my cup and we walked side by side to the elevator. He pressed the call button, reached for my empty hand with his, and threaded our fingers together as we waited.

After Valentine's weekend things had settled down. In fact, they'd settled *way* down. No more games were played, which was great. We saw each other daily, ate together as much as we could. We went to the gym together, library, studied together—all good things...

We spend a ton of time together. Sometimes we'd kiss. But mostly we talked.

However, there was one change in particular about which I felt some confusion, and I didn't know how to bring it up as a topic for discussion. During our first week officially together, he'd made silly sexual innuendos, puns, and witticisms. The more I was around him, the more they seemed habitual, unconsciously done. I'd been flustered at first—mostly because of the mental imagery they'd conjured—but just as I was growing used to this habit, he'd stopped.

He still flirted with me—at least I thought it was flirting—and we still kissed, but gone were the porn jokes and rhymes about copulation and masturbation.

I didn't know how to broach this subject. Should I just say, *Hey, you know what I miss? Your sex jokes.*

So I waited, looking for a natural segue for the conversation.

"Are you nervous?"

I shook my head. "No. Just sleepy."

"We can try to go back to sleep after."

I considered the likelihood that I'd be able to go back to sleep after a cup of coffee and backflips.

Meanwhile, the elevator dinged. The doors slid open and I was surprised to see a group of girls revealed, all dressed in club attire. Among the pack was Gail, the blonde who'd been spreading false rumors about Dara having an abortion several weeks ago. She'd also been the one to tell me about Greg and Vanessa's break up.

As soon as the girls saw us, their chatter abruptly ended. Seven pairs of eyes bounced back and forth between us for a protracted moment, nobody making any move to leave the elevator.

"Are you going down?" Greg asked, releasing my hand to hold the door. "Or are you getting off?"

"I'd go down with you," one of the girls said, drawing a few giggles.

"Then you'd be sure to get off," another slurred, making the rest of them laugh, this time in earnest.

"You're all soused," Greg said with no judgment. "You didn't drive, did you?"

And that's when I noticed their movements were sloppy as well as the smell of cigarette smoke and liquor wafting towards us. I recognized several of them as they filed out. I didn't know if they recognized me because they seemed to only have eyes for Greg.

Except Gail. I met her gaze and gave her a small smile. She didn't return it.

Gail stepped forward, her gait was unsteady. She was obviously drunk. "What are you two up to so late?"

I sensed Greg stiffen beside me when she spoke. I

glanced at him, found him glaring at Gail with unfettered loathing.

"Stuff and things." Greg waited until they'd all exited and then ushered me forward with a hand on my back.

"Couldn't sleep?" She pressed, narrowing her eyes. "The dorm beds aren't really made for two people."

"Thank you for sharing your opinion, I'll be sure to write about it in my diary."

"You have a diary?"

"I'll file it under, *Fuckwit-opinions no one cares about.*" His cool delivery made me wince on her behalf and I heard a few of the girls gasp. I didn't think she'd appreciate the sympathy in my expression, so I kept my eyes on the floor of the elevator as the doors slid closed.

As we descended I heard Greg mutter under his breath, "Rank, rump-fed harpy."

I twisted my mouth to the side and I considered him. "Another Shakespearean insult?"

"Yes," he responded instantly, nearly growling.

I lifted my eyebrows and said nothing. Obviously he wasn't Gail's biggest fan.

He appeared to struggle for a few moments before admitting, "This might be awkward for you to hear, but that girl—the blonde with the face like a frog—was very unkind to Vanessa when we broke up. She spread some nasty rumors, and I wish she were a man so I could call her out for it."

"She spread rumors about your ex-girlfriend?" The only rumor Gail had told me about Vanessa —which turned out to be fact—was that she and Greg had broken up.

He nodded tightly, his mouth curved in an unhappy line. "Ignorant bullshit, stupid stuff. But there's no reason to kick someone while they're down."

I surveyed his face, the drawn, stressed quality around his eyes. "If you want to talk about it, about..." I paused, hoping my intentions would be interpreted as supportive rather than prying. "If there's anything you want to talk about—your break up with Vanessa included—I hope you know you can talk to me."

"Thanks." He gave me a half smile, his expression clearing. "I'm afraid I wasn't very fair to her, and I... I lament that she was hurt."

"She seemed nice."

Even as I said the words—though they were honest—I felt a nonsensical sting of jealousy when he agreed, "She is nice."

I gave him a flat smile, then glanced away. I didn't know what I was doing. This conversation was weird and uncomfortable. Discussing his ex-girlfriends, and I assumed he had more than one, wasn't something I wanted to do.

Luckily the elevator doors opened, giving me a reason to move away from him and the topic.

"I'll go take a quick look around, make sure you don't have an audience." Greg walked past me, handing me his cup, his long stride carrying him to a hall that housed study rooms and led to an atrium at the other end of the building.

I placed both our coffee cups on a table near the periphery and examined the space. The lobby looked larger when empty, I estimated I had about forty feet of usable space. The floor was covered in compact carpet which would do nicely for a simple backflip. I toed off my slippers and removed my sweatshirt as Greg reappeared.

"There's a bunch of those vampire role players at the south end, but as long as we keep to this side we should be fine." He rubbed his hands together.

"Vampire role players?" I wrinkled my nose, confused by his words. "What are you talking about?"

"You know, those kids who dress up like vampires, they elect a king, they have court—very serious business."

"How many are there?"

"Fifty or so."

"Fifty? Do they bite each other?" Now I was curious.

"How should I know? Do I look like a vampire?"

I stretched my arm behind my head, narrowing my eyes on him. "Are you pulling my leg?"

"No. After you do your backflip we'll go take a look. Learn all their vampy secrets." He wagged his eyebrows. "Like, how do they shave with no mirrors, and how do they get blood stains out of bedclothes."

I turned away from him, shaking my head. "Okay, how many flips do you want to see?"

He took a step forward and stood at my shoulder. "How many can you do?"

"I don't know," I answered honestly, "I've never tried to see how many I can do in a row."

"Okay, three?"

"Sure."

I turned, pushed off with my legs, and did three backflips in quick succession, bouncing on my feet twice at the end of my short demonstration.

"Bloody hell!" he said, his mouth open, staring at me like I had super powers. "What else can you do?"

I smiled at his astonishment, proceeded to do a handstand, held it for a beat, and then walked on my hands, my body a stiff, straight line, my bare feet pointed.

"You're like a ninja! My girlfriend is a ninja!"

I tried not to laugh as it would interfere with my balance, or think too much about his use of the word *girlfriend*, but then succumbed to it, ending my walking handstand with a cartwheel.

Greg peeled off his sweatshirt, leaving him in a black Run DMC band t-shirt, and tried to do a handstand. It wasn't bad, but his height worked against him. His shirt fell to his chest and he wobbled, his long legs wavering in the air. I walked over to him and unthinkingly placed my hands on his bare stomach and back, helping him find his center of gravity.

"Point your toes, and imagine that you're a pole, perfectly straight." I was impressed I was able to keep my touch disinterested, though I longed to trace and explore his skin.

"I'm a pole, I'm a pole," he chanted. "I'm a pole… I wish someone would dance on me."

I snorted again, stifling my giggles by clamping my mouth shut. After a few more seconds, he fell inelegantly to the side, grinning at me from his spot on the floor.

"You make it look easy," he said, making no attempt to

disguise the wonder in his eyes or voice.

I liked the way he was looking at me, like I was special. I'd never been one for showing off. Competition was about skill and art, merit and talent, not about ego or unnecessary grandiose displays. But, strangely, I wanted to show off for Greg. I wanted to strut.

"You want to see something neat?" I asked, already crossing the lobby. The ceiling of the room was slanted, giving the room a breezy, open feel. At its shortest side, the walls were twelve feet; at its tallest they were at least twenty.

"*Something else*? You mean there's more?" He made no move to stand up, just watched me with wide eyes as I stood in the corner where the wall was tallest.

"I can touch the ceiling." I grinned at him.

His squinty eyes told me he didn't believe me. "With what?"

"What will you give me if I can touch the ceiling, with my hand?"

"I'll give you a big, fat diamond ring."

I rolled my eyes, doubting this promise for obvious reasons, and said, "Deal."

I turned, braced my hands on either side of the corner, and jumped. I then proceeded to climb the smooth surface, bracing my hands, knees, and bare feet against the walls.

When I was halfway to the top, Greg called, "Okay, point made. Come down."

"I'm almost there, I can do it."

"I believe you. Come down." I could tell from the

direction of his voice he was directly beneath me. I could also hear a new edge in his tone, a mixture of anxiety and irritation.

I ignored him, because I could do it, and instead methodically climbed the last five feet, touched the ceiling, then carefully began my descent. When I was eight or so feet from the ground, I felt large hands close around my waist and pull me from the corner. My arms—which weren't all that tired—automatically wrapped around Greg's neck as I turned my smiling face towards his.

He was not smiling.

I caught a glimpse of his austere frown as he set my feet on the ground, right before he wrapped his fingers around my jaw and neck and brought his mouth to mine. Unlike our previous kisses, this kiss wasn't patient; no prelude, or gentle nipping, or teasing. He was rough and unrelenting, using his teeth in ways I wouldn't have expected, but which caused an increase in both my body temperature and blood pressure.

Basically, he backed me into the corner, kissed the hell out of me, and made me hot and agitated.

And when he lifted his head, sucking and biting my bottom lip, I was left gasping for air. I could climb a wall without breaking a sweat, but after being kissed by Greg Archer I felt like I'd sprinted a mile.

"I want to say and do dirty things to you." His voice was heavenly sinful, growly and demanding. Greg's hands were still at my neck, his thumbs now pressing against my collar bone. "But I also want-"

"What kinds of dirty things?" I asked breathlessly,

realizing I'd gripped his t-shirt in tight fists. My heart skipped a beat, urgency in my veins, and my under-used imagination took this idea of dirty things and ran with it. "Be specific."

Greg huffed a small laugh, staring at me with heavy-lidded eyes. "You didn't let me finish. I was going to say, but I also want to bind you in bubble wrap, lock you away, and keep you safe."

That sounded immeasurably less fun than the dirty things.

I swallowed, about to voice this thought, but he interrupted me with another kiss.

This was the kind of kiss I'd grown to expect. A lingering, sweet kiss; one with extreme consideration, every movement and shift precious, as though he were committing them and me to memory. He breathed me in, his chest pressing against mine, and I melted.

It was lovely. He was lovely. But I still wanted to ask him about the dirty things. I wanted him to elaborate, in great detail, perhaps with some hands-on demonstrations. The farthest my imagination had got was us naked, standing like this... and then it didn't know what to think next. I had no experience with the kinds of *dirty things* he was referring to, but I was pretty sure they would be fun.

And yet... the idea of these unknown *dirty things* were also kind of scary, too.

Maybe he sensed my restlessness, because he retreated an inch and whispered against my mouth, "Fiona."

"Yes?" I didn't open my eyes, but I did hold my breath.

His fingers moved to my shoulders, down my arms, and

gathered my hands in his. I opened my eyes as he brought my knuckles to his lips and turned my hand.

Greg placed a soft kiss on the inside of my palm, saying, "We have forever, Darling. No need to climb the walls."

***

MADDIE, THE VERY sweet redhead on my floor, was one of the vampire role players. We spied her among the group after I finished my acrobatics and I'd recovered from Greg's kisses.

Well… recovered enough to walk in a straight line. I didn't think I'd ever truly recover.

We didn't lurk for an extended period of time, just long enough for me to assuage my curiosity and spot her sitting with a tall, blond guy. He was dressed in all black, and wore a cape. She was dressed in all black, and wore a mask.

But I was 99% sure it was Maddie because of her distinctive hair.

Vampire role-playing, or any real-life role playing, was a new concept for me and I found I was voraciously curious about it. So much so that when I spotted Maddie in the kitchen a week later, washing her dishes, I marched up to her and said, "I need to talk to you," in a way that sounded entirely too demanding.

Her eyes widened, her expression the perfect caricature of a deer caught in headlights.

When I saw I'd startled her, and maybe also worried her, I softened my tone and gave her a sheepish smile. "Sorry, I mean, if you have a minute, I'd like to ask you about something."

She visibly relaxed, releasing a nervous sounding chuckle. "You startled me for a minute, Fiona. I was like, *Oh shit! What did I do?* You're kind of scary."

I laughed and winced. I hadn't been called scary in years. When I was a competitor, my teammates said I could be scary, something about my game-face and demeanor must've screamed *don't fuck with me*. It wasn't purposeful, just a side effect of intense concentration.

"Do you have a minute?" I ensured my tone was gentle.

"Yes. Certainly. Go ahead."

I grabbed a towel and picked up her saucepan, drying it as I studied her. "So, last week, I was in the lobby in the early morning and think I saw you at the south end."

Maddie dropped the serving spoon she was washing; it hit the metal sink with a clatter and her eyes cut to mine. "Umm…"

"Or I saw someone who looked like you. Maybe it was someone else." It wasn't someone else, but I wanted to give her an out if this conversation made her uncomfortable.

Neither of us said anything for a long moment. She picked up her spoon, continued washing it, giving me side eye every few seconds.

When it was the cleanest spoon in the history of spoons, she asked haltingly, "What did you see?"

"You were—or the girl I thought was you was—sitting next to a guy in a black cape, talking. A bunch of other people, all dressed in black, were clustered in either pairs or small groups. Then there was this guy in a red cape who was sitting on a chair that looked like a throne."

I watched her chest rise and fall, her eyes stared forward like she was remembering something, or deep in thought. "What do you want to know?"

"Nothing specifically, I guess. I'm just curious."

Her gaze connected with mine and she searched my face. "Just curious?"

"That's right."

"No one put you up to this?"

"Put me up to this? What do you mean?"

"You're not making fun of me?"

"Why would I make fun of you?"

"Because dressing up like a vampire and pretending to be one is weird."

I stared at her for a beat, then said, "And hiding in your dorm room for the entire first semester of your freshman year is weird. And never seeing live TV or eating macaroni and cheese before the age of eighteen is also weird. So what? Everyone is weird."

The lines around her mouth and eyes softened. "You never had macaroni and cheese before going to college?"

"Never. Or hotdogs. Or fried chicken."

"Okay, that is weird," she laughed.

I laughed, too, glad the tension had been broken. "I'm curious. Truly, that's it. Greg said you all were doing vampire role-playing, and I-"

She cut me off with a strained sounding whisper. "What? Greg? Greg Archer? Greg knows?"

I placed my hand on her arm and squeezed; Fern did this to people when they became irrational. She said touching people was a good way to anchor them to the present and pull them out of their own head.

"Calm down. He and I were in the center lobby. We weren't spying, just checking to see if anyone else was around."

"He probably thinks I'm a freak." Maddie covered her face with her hands, then seemed to remember they were wet. She pulled the towel from my grip and dried her face off.

I decided to say, "I doubt he thinks you're a freak." Rather than, *I doubt he noticed you* or *I doubt he knows who you are*. Based on her dreamy expression a few weeks ago, when she'd discovered Greg and Vanessa had split, and her reaction now, I figured neither of those statements would ease her discomfort.

Maddie eyeballed me, her lips pinched together. Meanwhile I tried to give her an encouraging smile. I was pleased to see her relax by degrees, but felt a spike of something unpleasant when she shook off my hand.

"What were you and Greg doing in the lobby?"

I opened my mouth to respond with the truth, that I was demonstrating backflips and handstands, but something about her tone made me pause. I remembered Fern's earlier warning, about *other girls*.

So I lied. "I had a chemistry test last week. We went to the lobby to study so we wouldn't wake anyone up."

Maddie lifted a single eyebrow. "That's not what Gail said."

I stiffened, instinctively taking a full step away. Before I could form a response, Maddie crossed her arms over her chest and challenged, "No offense, but what are you thinking?"

"What do you mean?" My stomach felt abruptly sour, but I managed to school my expression.

"With a guy like Greg, every girl, every woman out there is your competition. He's insane levels of handsome—I mean, he's fucking hot as sin, and that accent—plus he's wicked smart, he used to be in the Marines for Christ's sake. He's every girl's wet dream. Do you really think it's a good idea to have Greg Archer be your first boyfriend?"

"Who said he was-"

"Dara told me he's always over since he split with Vanessa. And she said you've never had a boyfriend, and that you're really inexperienced." Maddie's voice held concern and sympathy, and her eyes were loaded with pity. "Do you really think you'll be able to keep his interest? When every girl out there is going to be trying to steal him from you? You're dooming yourself to heartbreak."

I stalled by pulling my eyes away and inspecting Maddie's dishes. I realized she thought she was doing a nice thing. She thought she was warning me to be careful with my heart. I should have thanked her for the concern and politely excused myself.

I should have.

But I didn't.

Because one thing being around Greg had taught me about myself was I enjoyed debating with people, especially when people are wrong.

So I said, "Your logic is flawed."

She snorted, turning her attention back to the sink and her very clean serving spoon. "Really? How so?"

"First of all, you're assuming women—or most women—intend to *steal* men from other women. You paint a very unflattering picture of women—sneaky, underhanded, selfish—and I don't think that's the case. I don't think most women behave that way or have those thoughts. Most women are not conniving."

Her gaze flickered to mine then back to her spoon. "Isn't that what you did to Vanessa?"

I shook my head and said, "No. I didn't." And I refused to dignify her statement with any additional explanation. Instead I continued, "And the other part of your logic that isn't accurate is your assessment of Greg. Greg is a person, not a spoon, or a saucepan, or a tea cup. He can't be stolen. Men aren't stolen. They're responsible for their own actions and decisions—staying with a woman is a decision. Straying or leaving is a decision. You make it sound like men are mindless, powerless to temptation."

She snorted. "In my experience, they are."

"Then you've known only weak men. And weak men deserve conniving women."

Maddie didn't look at me, but everything about her demeanor—the unhappy curve to her mouth, the prideful tilt of her chin, the jerky movements of her hands—told me I'd struck a nerve. I stared at her profile, waiting for her to respond. She didn't. Instead the silence grew awkward and unwieldy.

So I sighed, because I was sad. I'd liked Maddie, I still did, and I'd hoped we could be friends. But now I doubted it was possible. I pulled my fingers through my short hair and walked around her, realizing there was nothing more to say.

I was halfway to the door when she asked, "Are you going to tell everyone about me? About... what you saw?"

I turned and shook my head. "No."

"Then why were you pumping me for information?"

"Was I? I thought I was just asking you a question."

"Please." She rolled her eyes. "Stop with the innocent act. No one believes it."

I shrugged, recognizing the futility of my words before they were spoken, but needing to say them regardless. "I don't gossip, Maddie. If I want information, I go to the source. I'm not interested in rumors, only the truth."

***

GREG FOUND ME that evening curled up on my bed, staring out the window. I didn't give much credence to Maddie's claims—about Greg being lured away from my pathetic and inexperienced arms. I reasoned I wasn't interested in being with someone who could be stolen. Yet, a bitter kind of melancholy settled over my head and heart, making me crave the comfort of my pillow and covers.

"Are you sick?"

I turned at the sound of his voice, the familiar and lovely tight airiness in my chest making me sigh. He filled the doorway, his hands braced against the outside of the frame as his eyes moved over me, shaded with concern and affection.

"No." My lips tugged to the side and I reached my hand out to him. "I'm not sick. Will you lay with me?"

"I thought you'd never ask." He launched himself into the room, toeing off his shoes, and laid next to me on top of the covers.

"You can get under—under the covers—if you want. It's warmer."

"I'll bet it is." He kissed my nose as I turned completely around to face him, then leaned away, studying me and *not* taking me up on my under-the-covers offer. "What's wrong? Something is wrong."

I stared at him for a beat, then shrugged and answered honestly, "I think I'm lonely."

He cupped my cheek. "Lonely? Have I been neglecting you?"

I grinned at Greg's stricken expression and covered his hand with my palm. "No. Not at all. I see you every day. How could you be neglecting me?"

"I could sleep outside your door, keeping would be suitors *and* loneliness at bay."

I giggled. "That's not it. What I mean is, I think I miss my sister."

He blinked once, the lines of concern around his eyes softening with understanding. "You miss having a gal pal."

"I think so. Fern is wonderful, but she's not here very often, and I doubt she'll come back next year. I'm getting better at putting myself out there. I met a few girls on the floor who I thought…" I frowned, unable to complete the sentence aloud because I wasn't going to discuss my unpleasant Maddie run-in with Greg. "I think I just need to be patient."

Greg examined me for a beat, neither frowning nor smiling. At length, he rolled away, stood, walked to my door, shut and locked it. He paused, his hand hovering on the door knob. I lifted to my elbows to watch him. When he turned, the emotion behind his gaze startled me. I didn't know what it meant, but it appeared to be serious.

I slowly eased backward, my head connecting with my pillow. He stalked to the bed, tugging his sweatshirt over his head and discarding it to the floor.

My heart was beating triple time as he lifted the covers and climbed beneath. I scootched over, to give him more room, but he reached for my body and easily pulled me to the center of the bed. He climbed over me, his hips between my legs, hovering. He kissed me.

Greg's limbs tangled with mine, his long torso hot and hard above. His impressive shoulders and arms bracketed mine, caging me. Even though he braced most of his weight on his hands, he was solid and heavy.

At roughly 5'2", I'd never been a tall person. Yet—for whatever reason—I'd never thought of myself as small. Maybe because I'd always considered myself to be strong. I'd never wanted to feel small, never craved it.

However, in that moment, I did feel small. He was everywhere. Greg, his body, his presence, had never been so overwhelming. I felt delicate, but not in terms of being breakable. Rather, delicate in terms of being treasured and desired.

The being desired felt good—heart-soaring, belly-twisting, fever-inducing good—but also unsettling.

Admittedly, maybe my sudden sense of being small was

also due to the potential of being overpowered, dominated. Even if I'd been six feet, I suspected my thoughts and feelings would have been the same. I doubted he intended to intimidate me, but there it was. His strength, size, and maleness; his brain, background, and experiences; everything about him was intimidating.

I lifted my hands and tentatively placed them on his shoulders, telling myself to relax. And the longer we just kissed, our bodies moving and arching together in rhythm with our shared heartbeat, the more I did relax.

After a time, however, I grew restless again. Even though I still felt dominated and small, I wanted to do more than *just* kiss.

My touches grew bolder. I slid my hands down his chest to the hem of his shirt. I slipped my fingers into the band of his jeans. His hips jerked forward, trapping my hands between us, and pressing his hard length to my center.

My eyes flew open and an involuntary shudder passed through me. I opened my mouth, wanting to say something, but unable to speak.

Greg dipped his head to the side, breathing heavily against my neck, his words ragged. "Fe, you need to move your hands."

I gasped, because his hips shifted and mine rocked forward in a mindless response. The friction made everything about his solid, heavy, hot domination feel incredibly necessary, and then terrifying. And then necessary again.

"Ah… fuck." He tensed, holding his breath for several seconds. He rolled off of me, pushing the covers away but making no move to stand. His elbows were planted on his knees, his head in his hands, and I watched the rise and fall of his breaths.

Meanwhile I felt overheated, agitated, and… needy. I was sweating and my hands were shaking. I needed him to say something.

"Greg?"

"Give me a minute."

I nodded, even though he couldn't see me, and covered my face with my hands. I rubbed my eyes with my fingers and smiled, because this had definitely been a new experience. A thrilling, exciting, terrifying new experience. I folded my hands over my stomach and stared at the ceiling. My smile grew and I laughed lightly, feeling joy.

Greg twisted and peered at me, his left eyebrow lifted. When he saw my expression, his answering grin was hesitant and confused.

"What's so funny?"

"Nothing. Nothing is funny."

His eyes narrowed, but he was still smiling.

I laughed again and added, "Everything is serious."

He wrinkled his nose in suspicion, likely because I was caught in a fit of giggles, and turned completely toward me. His fingers dug into my sides and I jerked forward in response, gasping.

"Gah! That tickles!"

"But does it seriously tickle?"

I couldn't breathe, my body twisting in ticklish spasms,

made sensitive with pent up desire. "Yes, yes it seriously tickles! Stop! Please. Please stop!"

He did, kneeling on the bed, hovering over me with his crooked grin, his eyes bright and happy.

"Face the window, Fe. It's time to cuddle." Greg stretched beside me, over the covers, and nudged my shoulder, encouraging me to turn.

"Is this serious cuddling?" I teased. "Should I take notes?"

"Yes and yes. You should always be taking notes when we're together. I'm a consistent source of how to do everything right."

I snorted and he poked me through my covers. "Do you need to be seriously tickled again?"

"No!"

"Okay then. Simmer down." He wrapped his arm around me, his chest to my back, his chin at the crown of my head. We lay together for several minutes in cozy silence, both of us releasing heavy sighs of contentment.

As we snuggled, I realized I was happy, too. I'd been sad when he arrived, I'd been lonely. I didn't feel lonely now.

This thought made me frown at the window.

Certainly, my depth of feelings for Greg were due in part to the instant and undeniable attraction between us, the inexplicable and intangible sense of rightness the instant I laid eyes on him. Instead of dissipating, this attraction persisted, had grown and multiplied, fostered by conversation, respect, and laughter.

Every day, every moment we spent together was

building toward... something.

I was practical enough to be concerned by this realization. I couldn't allow Greg to become my whole world. I needed friendships. He'd chased my melancholy away with his kisses and touches, and of course I'd enjoyed every minute of it. But reason told me it would be a mistake to allow anyone—even Greg—to be the master of my happiness.

It wouldn't be fair to him, to burden him with all of my woes, wishes, and conversation.

And it wouldn't be fair to me.

Part 6: What's the difference between a ninja and an empty room?

"FAVORITE FOOD?"

"Soup. I love soup."

I lowered my gaze to the red and white checkered tablecloth, barely resisting the urge to pick wax off the old Chianti bottle currently being used as a candle holder. I didn't know how or when Greg had discovered this quaint Italian restaurant twenty minutes from the University, but I was glad he had. The food was awesome and the ambiance was singular and romantic. Manganiello's Italian Restaurant was a vast improvement over the Olive Garden.

Tonight was technically our first date, our first meal together not in the dorms or school café. He was in a suit, therefore I was having difficulty forming sentences, or breathing, or swallowing.

"What kind?"

"All kinds."

"All kinds?"

"Yes."

"Even lentil?" He sounded and looked shocked, appalled even.

I pressed my lips together to keep from laughing; apparently, trying not to laugh was my default expression when speaking with Greg. "I've been known to enjoy lentil soup, yes."

"Lentil soup is disgusting. It's the exact same texture as brains."

I lifted an eyebrow at this characterization of lentil soup. "And you know this how?"

"Stop changing the subject, why do you like soup so much—including, but not limited to, brain soup?"

I sighed, though it was a smiley sigh because I was enjoying his quick-witted irascibility. "I guess because soups are the food equivalent of a warm hug."

And just like that, his judgmental expression cleared. "Nice." He nodded his approval, giving me a quick smile before continuing his barrage of first date questions. I got the impression he'd been saving them up. "Okay, favorite ice cream?"

And just like that I was imagining Greg licking ice cream. My chest tightened. I cleared my throat, averted my eyes, and reached for my water.

Now late-April, we'd spent over two months kissing, touching over clothes, and cuddling. Maybe light caresses on my stomach and back. And not very often—twice a week, three times if I were lucky.

I thought about Hivan and Dara and their constant physical encounters. Greg and I were their opposite. They never spoke except to scream at each other. Greg and I spoke constantly and about almost everything under the sun—current events, history, philosophy, books, movies, hopes, dreams—and conversing with him felt akin to breathing, natural and necessary.

I'd learned he wanted to be a petroleum engineer, to keep accidents like the Exxon-Valdez disaster from happening again. I learned he was passionate about the environment, eradicating poverty and the resulting hunger and homelessness.

Yet we hadn't made it past second base.

We were taking things slow. Really, really slow. Molasses slow. Tectonic plates slow. Erosion slow. At first the slowness had been comforting, reassuring.

But now, I was fixating.

Little things about him had become oddly erotic and distracting. The way he pursed his mouth when he whistled, or how he'd stroke his bottom lip with his thumb when he was concentrating. His hands were a frequent source of thought derailment; sometimes I'd catch myself staring at his fingers and knuckles, and I'd lose my breath.

I was twisted in knots.

I couldn't quite look at him yet, still distracted by the mental image of him licking an ice cream cone, so I stated my response to the tablecloth. "No favorite."

"You don't have a favorite ice cream?"

"No. I'm an equal opportunity ice cream eater."

"We'll have to change that. Only fascists don't have a favorite ice cream." Lightning fast, he changed the subject. "I know you grew up without essentials, like a radio, but who is your favorite band? Or do you have one? I just realized I've never asked."

"Led Zeppelin." Finally (mostly) recovered, I met his gaze again.

He gave me a single eyebrow raise paired with, "Hmm... interesting. How did you get access to Led Zeppelin? Was it contraband smuggled in by a classic rock loving neighbor?"

"No, nothing so clandestine. My father has Led Zeppelin records and I used to listen to them over and over again when my mother was out of the house. He also has albums by The Beatles, Jimi Hendrix, The Yardbirds, Jefferson Airplane—that kind of music."

"All in vinyl?"

"Yes."

"That's rather impressive, actually. Favorite song?"

"Favorite Led Zeppelin song or just favorite song?"

"Your favorite song isn't by your favorite band?"

"Led Zeppelin is my favorite band because I love virtually all of their songs, they consistently write music I love. However, they didn't write the song I love the most."

"Which is?"

"A Kiss To Build A Dream On."

His brown eyes shifted to the right, like he was trying to place the title. When his gaze moved back to mine it was ripe with curiosity. "Isn't that an older song?"

"Yes."

"I don't think I've ever heard it, I'll have to look it up. Why the love?"

"My grandfather used to play it on the piano and my grandmother used to sing it when I was little. Sometimes, when I would visit them in the summer, they'd play it on their record player and dance to it, the foxtrot I think, in the living room. The way they would look at each other..." I sighed and gave him a little shrug. "It's the perfect song."

He was studying me, his eyebrows slightly furrowed, but a lingering smile in his eyes. "How did they look at each other?"

"They looked at each other like they cherished each other, like they couldn't live without the other. It's what I've always surmised being in love looked like."

"How old were they, when they did this?"

"When I visited them they were seventy or eighty, I guess."

His mouth tugged upwards on one side. "Enduring love."

"Yeah." I nodded, because that's what it was.

"I wonder if it still exists, if it's possible."

I frowned, blinked at him. But before I could comment he asked, "Favorite Muppet?"

"Um, Beaker."

"Yes! Right answer. Favorite Muppet movie?"

"Muppets Take Manhattan."

"Ah, not the right answer, but I'll allow it only because it wasn't the crappy space one. Favorite TV show?"

"Right now?" I had to think about this because I'd just recently started watching popular television shows. Prior to college, my TV options were limited to VHS cassettes of old movies and cartoons. "Um… Seinfeld."

"Really? Seinfeld? I took you for more of a *Friends* aficionado." Greg said this with no trace of condescension, which made me wonder if his favorite TV show was *Friends*… I found that unlikely.

"I like *Friends*, I do. But the absurdity of Seinfeld feels more like real life, I'm not one for fantasy. I also like that the show is about normal looking people and everyday situations."

"Normal looking people?" Greg stole one of my asparagus spears and began munching on the tip. His elbows were on the table and he was leaning forward, giving me his full attention—as per usual.

The first time we'd eaten together was in a school café—the week after Valentine's Day—and every time since he'd stolen food off my plate. Usually my French fries. I stopped ordering French fries only to discover Greg was an indiscriminate food stealer. No matter what was on my plate, he was going to steal it.

At some point I was going to pile it high with jalapeno peppers just to see what he'd do.

"Yeah. Normal looking people. Every character, or actor, on *Friends* is too pretty. I can't suspend reality for people that good looking—again it's a fantasy. I keep thinking, where are their normal looking friends? Are they only willing to be friends with young, beautiful, thin people of average height? And why is their apartment so big? That's a huge apartment for New York." I shrugged. "It bothers me."

He lifted a single eyebrow at my explanation, but a small smile curved his lips as I finished. He stared at me, the little smile affixed to his mouth.

I took a bite of my pasta, chewed, swallowed, and still he stared.

When he didn't speak after my second bite I prompted, "What?"

Greg shook his head quickly, as though he were coming out of a daze. "Nothing." His eyes lowered to the table, he was hiding them from me, and still he smiled.

"No, what is it?" I reached for my water, but didn't take a sip.

With obvious reluctance he lifted his eyes. Greg was still smiling, but his features were shaded with unmistakable melancholy. "I think, after facing death, seeing it, touching it, it's difficult to turn your brain off to the farcicalities of fantasy."

I blinked rapidly and heard my glass clunk as it hit the table. My death—or how close I'd come to it—wasn't something I was ready to talk about in serious terms with anyone, not even Greg. But this was the closest he'd come to discussing his time in the military, a topic I was ferociously curious about.

I chose my next words carefully, wanting him to elaborate, but not wanting to push. "What makes you think so?"

His smile grew into a knowing grin. My heart fluttered.

That smile...

Yes, Greg was tremendously attractive. Yet the more time we spent together the more his physical "flaws" came into focus. Discovering the existence of his imperfections surprised me, mostly because they were paradoxically both obvious and obscured.

As an example, Greg had a burn scar on the right side of his neck, under his jaw, and the lower half of his ear. After I noticed it, I realized his smile was crooked because of it; he must've lost some muscle mobility due to the burn. When I detected the scar for the first time I wondered why I hadn't seen it straight away, it was so obvious.

I think his smiles affected me so much because of the depth of the person behind them. He was... a force. Often overwhelming. Always captivating. Crooked or not, scarred or not, his grins were lethal, made my neck hot and my stomach flip—Every. Single. Time.

He didn't take the bait, instead opting to change the subject. "What finals do you have next week?"

"Just two, P-chem and differential equations. The other three are either class projects or papers, and those are mostly done."

"That's glorious. I have six."

"Six? Six exams?" I'm sure I looked horrified.

"Yes. Starting tomorrow, I shant sleep for a week. I've been procrastinating. I haven't finished my research paper on bio fuels. It's due on Monday."

"Let me know if I can help."

He shook his head mournfully. "Sadly, there is no help to be had. I've been distracted this semester and am paying the price now."

"I'm sorry."

"Don't be." His gaze moved over me. His whisper of a smile felt secretive, meaningful as he added, "It was totally worth it."

We stared at each other, smiling. Me flushing with pleasure. Him grinning wider at my blush.

Still grinning roguishly, he asked, "Are you ready to get

out of here?"

I surveyed my plate and found I was full. "Yes. What's next on the agenda?"

"It's a surprise." He'd kept the plans for this evening top secret.

"Can I guess?"

He smirked and motioned for the waiter to bring us the bill. "You can try."

"A movie?"

His lips parted and he looked horrified. "A movie? Certainly not! What do you take me for? A pedestrian?"

The check was delivered to our table. I turned for my purse, but before I could take out my card he'd already settled the bill with cash, telling the waiter to keep the change.

I glowered at him. He answered my obvious displeasure by lifting an eyebrow and taking a drink from the vodka (neat) he'd been nursing all through dinner.

"Greg."

"Yes, Darling?"

"We didn't discuss how we would split the check."

"I wasn't aware it needed discussing."

"I would like to split it."

Greg shrugged, his lips pulling to the side, his tone that of a parent imparting a lesson. "Well you can't always have what you want."

A short laugh burst forth, but I was determined to press the point. "Expenses should be split."

"I don't like splitting things," he said as he stood, holding his hand out to me. "The maths are too hard for my brain."

"I'm being serious." He helped me with my coat and we

strolled arm in arm out of the restaurant. "I may not be the world's foremost expert on dating, but I do know money can't be a major point of contention, especially if one person carries the entire financial burden."

I was thinking of my parents. My father always worked outside the home and my mother was a homemaker. She always felt like she needed to ask permission before spending money on herself, like my father's check was *his* money. This was exacerbated by his requirement that she provide receipts for all purchases. I think it was part of what made her so volatile all the time, feeling like she had no control of her own destiny.

He opened the passenger side door to his truck, gazing down at me as though I were a curiosity. "Fe, in a relationship, money is one of many burdens. Are you proposing that people split all burdens, right down the middle?"

"Yes," I said, and thought about the feasibility of this approach as he shut my door and came around to his side. When he was settled in his seat, I clarified. "Well, insomuch as is feasible. I mean, some burdens aren't quantifiable. So I suppose, people should do their best to split things fifty-fifty."

"And, hypothetically, if we were to have children, would we have shifts? You have them for fifty percent of the day, I have them for fifty percent of the day? I worry about fifty percent of the issues? I help them with fifty percent of their homework? I do fifty percent of the grocery shopping?"

I conceded his point. "Like I said, some burdens aren't quantifiable, but money is."

"But—don't you see? Money isn't. Not really. Because a relationship is made up of many burdens, and the two people within the relationship have different strengths and weaknesses, abilities and talents."

"And your talent is having more money than I do?" I asked wryly.

He nodded once. "For now. But later, your talent might be having more money than I do. And therein lies the beauty of partnering off with another human."

"The beauty of human relationships is sharing burdens?"

"More or less. But burdens don't grow lighter if both people are contributing *equally*. Life isn't a fifty-fifty split, that's just being lazy. Burdens are weightless, worlds change, and love endures when both people are contributing their maximum."

I mulled this over; I could see his point, but it didn't strike me as terribly practical. Romantic? Yes. Optimistic? Absolutely.

But could this altruistic strategy actually work in real life? Doubtful.

His eyes flickered to mine as he pulled out of the parking lot. "I see my superior reasoning has not won you over."

"It's just that…" I twisted my hands together. "I think what you're suggesting is the ideal. But it's not very practical. Humans are fallible and selfish. They *are* lazy. And they so often take the road of least resistance. The idea of being at the mercy of another person's decisions, trusting that person with my bank account and the money I earn, feels like dooming a relationship to failure. Wouldn't it be better to split expenses from the start? So you don't have to rely on anyone else? Plus, if things don't work out, then you'd have to separate your finances. I've seen plenty of my friends' parents get divorced and money is always the biggest point of contention."

"Not the children?"

"No, interestingly. Unless child support is involved—so, again, money—then the kids factor into the equation in a big way. Just to be clear, I understand their perspective. Money puts food on the table and a roof over your head. There's nothing wrong with wanting to have money and the security it provides, which is why removing money from the relationship equation makes so much sense."

He shook his head. "I think the opposite is true. I think—unless you have some compelling reason to keep bank accounts separate—the separation of finances *just in case* dooms a relationship to failure. It's like each person already has one foot out the door, like those people who get married and think to themselves, *Oh, well if this doesn't work out, I can always get a divorce.*"

I smirked at him, amused by how riled up he was getting about this. Usually, when we debated, he was cool, witty, and irritatingly detached. This was fun.

"Well, it's true, you know. If a marriage doesn't work out, you *can* just get a divorce."

"Thank you for that, Duke of Obvious-shire."

My shoulders shook with silent laughter. I tried to hide my smile as the truck descended into a contemplative silence. I assumed he was thinking about my perspective as much as I was thinking about his. I loved being in his company, being with him, partially because we frequently debated. We were always discussing and challenging each other to view things from a new perspective.

This debate was just like any of the others we'd had, except I was usually the optimist and he was typically a staunch pessimist. I was having a good time being the devil's advocate for once.

I looked out the window and rubbed my fingers together. Even with the heat on full blast in the truck, my fingers were cold.

The passing cornfields were barren. It was too early to plant. The landscape was open and desolate, visible in shadow only because of the full moon. I saw we were just three exits away from the University. I didn't know what he had planned for the rest of the evening, but I hoped it included us making out in his truck.

"Here's the thing..." he started, stopped, then growl-grunted like he was frustrated. I turned to face him and his eyes cut to mine briefly before continuing, "I don't want that. I don't want a half-assed relationship with a life-partner who's looking to leave. I think you're right for the most part, humans are lazy and selfish. But—and I can't believe I'm the idealist in this conversation—I also think you're wrong. Take your grandparents, for example."

"My grandparents?"

"Yes. Did your grandmother work outside the home?"

"Not really. Just for a few years, after her kids were out of the house."

"And did your grandfather ever make her feel like his income wasn't equally hers?"

"No. He didn't. In fact, she was the bookkeeper in their marriage. She paid all the bills and gave *him* an allowance." I grinned because I recalled the conversation I'd had with my grandmother on the subject. She'd said women were better at balancing budgets because they're better at spending money.

"So, it's possible? It's possible to share *everything*, all burdens, including monetary ones? Be human, but not be selfish or lazy with your wife or husband or partner?"

"Yes. Of course it's possible, but-"

"No! No *but*!" He spoke over me. "Because if it's possible to have a partner who gives all of themselves without reservation, who looks forward to working and sacrificing for me just as I look forward to doing the same for her, who can't help but love ferociously, brutally, and unconditionally—and even perhaps without reason or sound judgment—that's what I want. Because that's how I plan to love in return."

I squinted at him, letting this idea of ferocious, brutal, sacrificing love take root. I wasn't ready to subscribe without more debate. "But that's what everyone wants, Greg-"

"I'm not talking about other people," he mumbled under his breath as I continued philosophizing.

"-just like everyone wants to be a millionaire, and have their own island, and be a rock star."

"And all of those goals are possible, if you work hard enough."

"Not necessarily. Even with the best of intentions, sacrifice, and hard work, some marriages fail. I'm convinced success—in anything—has four facets: one part hard work, one part talent, one part blind luck, and one part who you know."

"And I know you, and you know me. And maybe…"

I snapped my mouth shut and frowned, waiting for him to continue. Some element to his voice wasn't quite right.

My brain was having a hard time disengaging from debate inertia, but as I stared at him, at his profile, I recognized he was more invested in this discussion than was typical. Whereas I'd approached the topic as though it were just another one of our debates—dealing in hypotheticals, gross generalizations, and empirical data—looking at him now, I wondered if he'd been speaking with more specificity. *Not* hypothetically.

Greg gripped the steering wheel with white knuckles and glared in his rearview mirror. "Never mind."

"No. Not *never mind*. What were you going to say?"

I watched his Adam's apple bob as he swallowed. "Nothing interesting."

"Tell me."

He shrugged, pulling into the lot for our dorm, parking, and exiting the truck. I stared at his empty seat while he came around to my side and opened my door. I stood and sought his eyes. He gave them to me, but he was withdrawn.

I reached for his hand and threaded our fingers together before he could move away. "Greg, I thought we were debating."

"We were."

"Were we?"

"Yes."

"And not about us, but about society in general?"

His jaw ticked, and he gave me a smile that didn't quite reach his eyes. He adopted his driest tone as he replied, "Fe, we've been together for a while. I am very fond of you—despite your distressing pessimism about marriage— and would like to buy you dinner, from time to time, without you harassing me about splitting the check."

I thought about replying with, *As long as I can buy you dinner from time to time*, but thought better of it.

Instead, I stepped away from the car, shut the door, and reached for his hand. "Yes, please. That sounds really nice. Thank you."

The hard curve of his mouth softened and so did his eyes. We'd walked some distance toward the dorm when he asked, "What if I wanted to buy you dinner every Friday?"

"I guess I'll be eating well on Fridays, except for all the food you steal from my plate." I withdrew my student ID from my pocket and used it to open the security doors.

His earlier stoicism was eclipsed by a devilish smile. "I can't help myself, you make everything enticing."

I was about to echo his sentiment, that he made everything enticing, but we were interrupted by the sound of someone calling my name from behind us.

We both turned in unison, and my eyes landed on a woman some twenty feet away.

"What the...?" I took a step back.

"Fiona! Wait!" she called, being unnecessarily loud, splitting her attention between me and the cell phone pressed to her ear. She began yelling about tire chains and tow trucks to whoever was on the line.

"Who's that?" Greg asked, his eyes on my profile.

I gathered a deep breath and braced myself for... whatever came next.

"That's my mother."

***

I RAN MY wrists under the cold water, dried my hands, checked my reflection, reapplied my lipstick, and checked my reflection again. I unlocked the bathroom door and braced myself, conducting a mental walkthrough of the next forty-five minutes.

I used to have a fear of needles, a true phobia. I would pass out whenever I saw a syringe. Having cancer and having a needle phobia is like being a goalie and having a fear of balls.

My doctor suggested systematic desensitization as a way for me to overcome my fear. He sent me home with several syringes, telling me to hold them. That didn't go over well. I began having nightmares that someone would find the syringes and stab me while I slept.

Not helpful.

His next approach worked much better. Before each visit where blood had to be drawn—so, all visits—he told me to imagine going through the motions of having my blood taken. I imagined in my mind's eye walking into the hospital, waiting in the waiting room, being called back, sitting in the phlebotomist's chair, and having my blood taken.

Suddenly, my fear didn't feel quite so insurmountable.

Since then, I'd applied this technique many times, especially in stressful situations.

And so, I was applying this technique now.

I'll walk into the suite. I'll offer her something to drink. I'll find out what she's doing here and how long she's staying. I'll talk to her for ten additional minutes and then I will go to the bathroom. I will speak to her in ten-minute intervals, taking frequent trips to the bathroom until the tow truck driver arrives. Then I'll take her downstairs. I'll call her a cab. She will leave.

I gulped in one more breath for bravery, and walked out of the floor bathroom, down the hall, and into my suite area. I'd opted to escape to the central bathroom in the middle of the dorm floor rather than the suite bathroom. The sound of easy conversation met my ears, pleasant tones engaging in chit chat.

Fern was sitting at her desk painting her toenails, her feet propped up on the counter. Her gaze met mine briefly; it was saturated with sympathy.

Meanwhile, Greg was standing outside my dorm room, leaning against the wall and presumably facing my mother. I couldn't see her, she was hidden from view, and she couldn't see me either.

She was talking, "... you can imagine, the whole ordeal was very hard on me. We thought she was going to die, and the family burial plot didn't have spaces for her and her sister, so we had to try to purchase a different plot close by. Well, once we bought the gravesite, Fiona improved. So now we have this gravesite and it was a complete waste of money."

Greg issued me an impassive once over, and turned his attention back to my mother, his tone conversational. "You never know, perhaps Fiona will expire sooner than expected. She could get hit by a bus. Or maybe one of her cousins will meet an untimely end. If you think about it, having that extra gravesite is a good idea. Now, if she or her sister, or any of your nieces or nephews die unexpectedly, you're all set. Just think how easy the funeral arrangements will be."

I closed my eyes, uncertain if I wanted to laugh or cry. She was complaining about the gravesite again. Everywhere she went, every new person she met, she complained about the gravesite my parents had purchased, but was now of no use. I'd had the audacity to live, leaving them saddled with a superfluous gravesite.

"That's a good point..." came my mother's reply, and I knew she actually thought he'd made a good point. "I always say, when life gives you lemons, make lemonade. My sister's kid is always getting in trouble. I bet I could sell it to her."

I decided to never play poker with Greg because his expression didn't waver in the slightest at her words. Instead, he nodded earnestly, like this was an excellent idea, and added, "Is it a nice location? Does it have a view? If it has a view you should charge more for it. Also add some flowers, landscaping always improves property value."

I gaped at his profile.

I hadn't wanted to leave him alone with her. I'd worried she would... not embarrass me, per say. Rather, I was worried she would terrorize Greg.

When I saw her, I'd given him an out. I told him to run, run like the wind, escape her crazy. He'd steadfastly refused to leave, instead suggesting I go visit the bathroom because he was sure the seafood I'd had for dinner wasn't fresh.

I had no seafood for dinner.

But I still went to the bathroom.

"It does have a view. I hadn't thought of that." I heard her stand from my bed and her footsteps approach. "I wonder where Fiona is? I hope she didn't fall in the toilet."

Greg straightened from where he'd been leaning against the wall and did a double-take, as though he were just seeing me just now.

"Oh! Here she is, she just walked in."

Not a second later, my mother stuck her head out of my room and frowned at me. "Tummy problems? Do you have any baking soda? Or is it constipation?"

I'm going to be honest, I kind of wanted to die in that moment.

"No, mother. I'm fine. I just ran into someone in the hall from my chemistry class." The white lie slipped effortlessly out of my mouth. My childhood had been seasoned with white lies. I'd learned early on how to lie believably. I considered it a survival skill.

She drew herself up, looking offended. "You should have told them that your mother was visiting and you didn't have time to talk."

I nodded, giving her my best apologetic smile. "You're right. I should have. I'm sorry." Agreeing with her and apologizing were the two most reliable ways to avoid being screamed at.

"Apology not accepted. You know better."

I didn't respond right away. Instead, I lowered my eyes to the carpet and counted the paperclips under my desk. I'd spilled a box of paperclips earlier in the day and apparently had missed a few.

"Well, anyway... this whole day has been a disaster. I don't know why you wanted to go to school here. I think Iowa gets more snow than Maryland, if that's possible. I'm tired of the snow, I want to go someplace warm. But you and your father insist on these cold climates."

"I didn't know you were planning to visit," I said, hoping I sounded benignly interested rather than irritated.

"Yes, if we'd known, we would have ordered the sky to cease snowing." My eyes cut to Greg and I found him giving my mother a smile I'd never seen from him before. It was not a pleasant smile.

To my surprise, she chuckled, "I bet." She gave Greg an amused head shake and sighed. "Well, as soon as the new car arrives, I'm leaving. Your father has a conference in Chicago, that's the only reason I'm here. I waited two hours for you, Fiona. And now our opportunity to spend time together is gone."

I was spared having to respond because her cell phone rang; she answered it and held a finger up in the air, silencing me.

"What's that?" she yelled at the phone. "Oh... you're outside?"

My mother turned away from both of us, continuing her loud conversation in my room. Greg reached forward and pulled the door shut, immediately turning to me with a grimace.

"She's horrible," he whispered accusingly. "I thought you said your childhood was *fine*? That woman isn't fine. She's Satan."

I heard Fern half snort from behind me as I gave him a wane look. "Can we not discuss this now?"

"If not now, when?!" he demanded dramatically, clearly joking.

I pressed my lips together so I wouldn't laugh. If she came out here and saw me laughing she would assume the worst (she'd be correct) and I'd be on the receiving end of her temper tantrum.

I turned away from Greg—because the longer we stared

at each other, the more likely I was going to burst out laughing—and covered my mouth with my hand. I didn't even have a minute to pull myself together before she reappeared.

"Take me downstairs, Fiona. The new rental car is here."

I nodded dutifully, unwilling to meet Greg's eyes for fear he'd have me in a fit of giggles.

"Your rental car? What about the tow truck?" he asked, walking ahead of us and holding the door.

"Not here yet. I gave him Fiona's number, he'll call when he arrives and she can meet him to get the other car. Here are the keys." She held them out to me, I accepted them, glancing at Greg as we walked by.

He was scowling. Actually, he was scowling with intensity. His eyes shot sparks of irritation and fury at my mother's back. I watched with horror as he set his jaw, drawing himself up to his full height, his eyes half-lidded with brazen contempt. I knew him well enough to recognize he was about to throw down a gauntlet, or toss out a stinging insult, or both.

I caught his eyes, mine widened to their maximum diameter. I vehemently shook my head, mouthing *no, no, no!*

He opened his mouth, saying nothing, but giving me a pleading look.

Please, the look said. *Please let me set down your mother. Please let me harass her and make her cry. Please allow me to make her feel terrible about herself.*

I shook my head slowly, giving him a mournful smile.

He looked like he was ready to explode.

My smile grew less mournful.

"Fiona?"

I hadn't been paying attention to my mother, so I didn't

realize she'd stopped walking and was glancing between me and Greg.

"Coming, mother."

"It was fascinating to meet you, Mrs. Shepard," Greg called after us.

"You too, Gregory. Thank you for your thoughts on that troublesome property issue."

Greg hesitated, biting his lip—which meant he was trying to hold his tongue—but in the end he blurted, just before we walked into the elevator, "Thank you for Fiona. Your troublesome property issue notwithstanding, I'm glad she didn't die."

I glanced at my mother; she was watching Greg like he was strange. Eventually, she nodded faintly, stepping into the elevator and pressing the button for the lobby. I followed her, breathing a silent sigh of relief when the doors closed. We stood in silence as the car descended, and I began to hope no additional conversation would be forthcoming.

But just as the doors opened, my mother said, "You should hold on to that one. Don't let anyone steal him away."

I stiffened, frowning, uncertain if she'd spoken or if I'd imagined the words.

"Earth to Fiona, did you hear what I said?"

I quickly nodded, following her out of the lift. "Yes. I did."

"He's worth securing," she tossed over her shoulder. "You're lucky you met him before someone else snatched him up."

Part 7: What do you get when you cross a ninja?

I NEVER DID discover what Greg had planned as a surprise for our first date.

After my mother left, I went back upstairs and waited for the tow truck driver. Just as the man called, Greg showed up in my suite, looking scrumptious in pajamas and boots. He told me to hand over the rental car key. I changed while Greg went downstairs to deal with the man.

Greg didn't come back to my room. I waited for an hour and a half and was just about to walk to his room when he called me on the phone.

"Sorry I didn't come back up straightaway. I stopped by the boxes to check my mail." He sounded distracted.

"No problem. Do you want me to head over to your room?"

"No, don't do that. Sasquatch is here with a bird and, uh..." He hesitated and cleared his throat before continuing, "This week will be completely mad. I'm going to call it a night."

"Okay. For the record, I had a great time on our date."

"Even though I abscond with your food?"

"Yes. Even though you're a dirty food absconder." I paused, then added, "Sorry about my mother."

I heard him chuckle. "We shall discuss her Royal Horribleness at length tomorrow. I'm miffed you didn't tell me the truth about her. Is your father an ogre too?"

"No." I glanced at the clock, saw it was past midnight, and all of the sudden I was tremendously tired.

"Would you tell me if he were an ogre?"

"Probably not." I yawned and turned down my covers.

Greg was silent for a beat; I could tell he was thinking, considering his words. At length, he asked, "Seriously, why did you say your childhood was fine?"

I was glad he wasn't here, in my room, for this conversation. "Because it was fine. Like I said, I had a roof over my head, food, safety-"

"Yes, but a child requires more than the minimum, Fe. You deserved more than merely shelter, food, and safety. You deserve more than that now."

Inexplicably, my bottom lip trembled, so I bit it and closed my eyes.

"Fiona? Are you there?"

When I was quite certain I could keep the tears from my voice, I said. "Yes. I'm here. I'm just tired. How about we discuss her Royal Terribleness-"

"You mean her Royal Horribleness."

"Yes. Her Royal Horribleness, we'll discuss her tomorrow."

He hesitated again, but in the end he agreed.

However, I didn't see Greg the next day, or the day after that, or the day after that. It was the week of finals and I reasoned, as a junior, his schedule was likely crazy. Whenever I'd stop by his room he was gone—at the gym, library, computer lab. And several times I'd returned from class to learn he'd stopped by while I was out.

He left me short notes on my bed, just a few words scrawled on a post-it note,

Are you hiding from me? –Greg

I'll be at the computer lab in engineering all day, come find me if you have time. –Greg

Have you once again succumbed to the call of the hermit lifestyle? –Greg

I miss you. —Greg

I missed him, too. I missed our debates. I missed kissing him and touching him. I missed the cuddling. In truth, I pined for him and was verging on pathetic by day three.

And yet, the absence from each other was a good reminder I needed more people in my life.

Therefore, on day four, I looked up the martial arts club on campus and filled out the paperwork to join. On my way out of the student union I spied a flyer for a knitting group meet up over the summer; I grabbed one of the tear off numbers and resolved to go.

Perhaps invigorated by the idea of the knitting group and kung fu, I asked a girl in my differential equations class if she wanted to grab coffee after the final to celebrate. She agreed. So we grabbed coffee and she told me about her childhood, how she'd been raised in New Mexico but moved to Iowa when she was fifteen.

When the time came for us to part, we made plans to go out again when summer classes started in three weeks. She mentioned the possibility of a movie and I readily agreed.

I missed Greg. We'd spent nearly every day together since Valentine's Day; the time without him had been a shock to my system, but also a much-needed wakeup call. I needed friendships beyond Greg. Life happened, he was busy, and placing him firmly in the center of my universe was unfair to us both.

However, on day five, I came home to find three rocks on my desk and a card with a penguin on the front. Seeing it was from Greg, I did a little happy dance as I bounced into my room, reading his inscription.

Dearest Fiona,

I'm missing you dreadfully. It's been an age, I don't think you'll recognize me when next we meet. I've put on ten stone and lost all my hair. And an eye. I hope you fancy a fat bald man with an eye patch.

Come out with me on Friday. Finals will finally be over and it'll be time to celebrate. I'll pick you up at four. We'll do a first date do-over, eat at Manganiello's again, plus a new, improved surprise.

Also, FYI: Gentoo penguins mate for life. Whereas Adélie penguins prostitute themselves for rocks.

I'd like to be your Gentoo penguin.

-Greg

P.S. Unless you're open to a rock arrangement. If so, please find my first down payment enclosed.

***

I BOUGHT A new dress.

In a fit of restlessness, Fern and I decided to go shopping. It was her last week at the University. She'd decided to drop out after exams were over, move to Clearwater, Florida, and pursue her career as a Scientologist minister. I did my best not to dwell on her impending departure.

So we went to the mall.

The dress was black, and the flared skirt was much shorter than any I'd worn before. But the weather had turned almost nice, and Fern was adamant that the quality of my legs required showing off. I didn't disagree, as I'd often considered my legs to be my best physical attribute.

Fern informed me that she considered my eyes to be my best physical attribute. "They're soulful and sad, intelligent and welcoming. They make me want to give you a hug, and anticipate the hug I'll receive in return."

This earned her a delighted smile.

But then she quickly smacked my bottom and added,

"And your ass is your second best physical attribute. Work it, girl!"

"You are a goofball." I twisted away from her slap-happy hand and claimed a seat in the food court.

"What? Doesn't Greg ever compliment your bottom?" She took the chair across from mine.

I didn't answer, instead opting to roll my eyes. She wasn't deterred by my non-answer.

"He doesn't?" She sounded shocked. "What about when you two are having sex? Or is he not a talker?"

I held very still, hoping... hoping something, like the ground would open up or a dinosaur on a spaceship would magically appear. Unsurprisingly, the dinosaur let me down.

Disappointing dinosaur is... disappointing.

Eventually, I met Fern's eyes. She was staring at me with plain disbelief. "You two haven't...?"

I shook my head.

"But you've had oral sex?"

I shook my head.

"But he's used his fingers?"

I shook my head.

"Good God, what are you two waiting for?"

I laughed, my face falling into hands. "I don't know!" I wailed.

But I kinda did know, or at least I suspected... "I think he's trying to take things slow. We do a lot of... kissing."

"Necking. Making out."

"Yes. Exactly."

"He's worried about scaring you off? You think?"

I shrugged. "Maybe." Then I nodded. "Probably."

"Would he? Scare you off, I mean."

"At this point, no. I mean, I trust him. And I... I've never been in love before."

Fern rested her chin in her hands, giving me a dreamy smile. "First love..." then she sat up straight and snapped at me. "I know! You should suck on his finger!"

"Excuse me?"

"Suck on his finger. The middle one. If that doesn't work, try rubbing your bottom against his groin. And don't be subtle about it either. There's no way he hasn't had fantasies about your ass. Hell, *I've* had fantasies about your ass."

Fern cackled at her own joke and I reluctantly joined in. This conversation was both mortifying and liberating, and I wondered how I was going to make it through the next year without her.

***

UPON SEEING ME in my new dress, Greg's gaze lingered on my legs. It was hard to miss the appreciative gleam in his eyes. I took this as a sign of success.

But then he asked, "So... are you going to put on some pants?"

I glanced at my legs, then back at him. "What do you mean?"

"I'm assuming that's a shirt with a belt and, my poor darling, you've forgotten your pants." He ruined the effect by laughing at his own joke. He was a teasing teaser. I'd missed his teasing.

We'd been separated for the last week, and yet it felt like no time had passed. Everything was just as easy and comfortable as it had been before. Though we were perhaps a tad anxious to learn what the other had been up to over the last seven days.

Manganiello's was once again excellent. And this time I'd allowed Greg to pay for the meal without objection.

He'd done so with flourish, leveling me with a self-satisfied smirk when he handed over his credit card. I didn't care. I was just happy to see him smile. After a week without his company, my heart felt generous where he was concerned. Generous and greedy.

At present, I was gazing out the window, not really absorbing any true details of the passing scenery or the song playing over the stereo, thinking instead on my earlier conversation with Fern. Specifically, I was thinking about the logistics of sucking on Greg's middle finger. Should I do it now? Or should I wait until we were back at the dorms? And what could I expect as a result? Was sucking on a man's finger the universal green light for sexy times?

Because I was gazing out the window, I noticed a green highway sign telling me we were an hour from Chicago.

It took me several seconds to process what I'd read. When I did, I started, stiffening, and slid my eyes to the side. If Greg knew we were driving in the wrong direction, he made no outward sign.

I shifted in my seat. "I think we're going the wrong way."

"No," he said simply, not looking at me.

"That sign back there said we're going east."

"That's right."

I studied his profile, waited for him to comprehend that east was the opposite direction from the University. Again, he made no outward sign.

"Greg, that sign was for Chicago."

"I know," he said evenly.

I opened my mouth, closed it, feeling like I was missing something. We were quiet for several minutes while I tried to figure out what was going on.

When I couldn't, I asked, "What's going on?"

He paused, like his instinct was to respond one way, and he was trying to subdue this instinct. "We're not going back to the dorms tonight."

Every muscle in my body tensed, my ability to breathe hijacked by the implications of this statement. In truth, I was blindsided.

I wasn't opposed to the implications. Obviously I wasn't since, just moments ago, I'd been sitting here, plotting how and when to suck his finger into my mouth. But I was surprised.

I moved so that my back was against the door and I was facing him, attempting to sound casual. "Oh."

His gaze flickered to mine. He grinned, it was quickly suppressed. "Fern packed you a bag."

"Fern packed me a bag," I parroted, nodding. "Well, that was nice of her."

"She's very helpful."

"Yes. Helpful." I was glad that the interior of his truck was dark because I was most assuredly scarlet from the top of my head to my toes.

Greg was biting his bottom lip; I could tell he was trying not to smile. He also appeared to be battling with himself. I could almost see a devil on one shoulder and an angel on the other.

We drove in silence for several long minutes, my mind racing. I clasped and unclasped my hands in my lap, twisting my fingers, my heart jumping around wildly. I was excited. I was also nervous.

But—surprisingly—I wasn't worried and I wasn't irritated he hadn't discussed this step with me ahead of time. Maybe I should have been, but I wasn't.

"You're very quiet." His tone was desert dry, which was how I knew he was trying to keep the smile out of it.

"So are you." I was pleased with how even, unaffected I

sounded.

"I was just thinking, I wonder what Fern packed for you. I can't wait to see."

A new bloom of warmth spread from my chest to my fingertips. This was possibly the most sexually flirtatious he'd been with me in over a month, and it was about damn time. It occurred to me that perhaps he'd been suppressing the witty sexual innuendos since early March because he thought they made me uncomfortable.

I decided to test this theory... by trying to make him uncomfortable. I may have been an awkward seductress, but I was determined to be a seductress nevertheless.

I crossed my legs and shrugged, picking a piece of lint from my black dress. "Hopefully nothing."

I sensed him stiffen, watched his eyebrows pull low as though he were confused. "Pardon me?"

"I hope she packed nothing, except maybe a toothbrush."

He squirmed in his seat and was quiet for the rest of the drive.

Meanwhile I spent the time trying to hide my smile.

***

IMPROV.

That was the surprise.

Greg had secured tickets to an improv festival in Chicago. I think I laughed for three hours straight, my jaw and sides hurt. It was so funny that Greg eventually loosened up as well.

My comment in the car, meant to make him slightly uncomfortable, made a larger impact than I'd anticipated because his strange, meditative silence persisted. As well, he was more hands on than was typical—pulling me under his arm instead of holding my hand, rubbing my shoulders as we stood in line, kissing my neck when we were seated.

My theory—that he'd been holding back because he didn't want to push me out of my comfort zone—was confirmed in spades.

With each touch and kiss he took a step back and studied me, as though he were gauging my reaction. My reaction each time was to return his affection with affection, and to try to up the ante a hundred fold.

He placed his arm on my shoulders, I placed my hand on his butt. And squeezed.

He rubbed my back, I rubbed my bottom against his groin.

He kissed my neck. I brought his middle finger to my mouth, was able to suck on it for maybe three seconds before he pulled it out of my grasp and gaped at me like I'd lost my mind. He cursed, inspected our surroundings to see if anyone had been watching, and shifted in his seat like he was having trouble holding still.

I didn't care. The seed had been planted back in the car on the drive over. He'd definitely been teasing about staying in the city. He'd had no intention of spending the night with me. The surprise was the improv, not a night together.

As funny and enjoyable as the show was, I was disappointed.

When we stood to depart after the program and he drew me close to his side, I decided to push the matter.

"So, where is our hotel?"

His narrowed gaze slid to mine. He said nothing.

"Oh, I see. You were bluffing."

He stopped walking, also pulling me to a stop, and turned me to face him. His eyes made a quick survey of my upturned face and he stepped closer, forcing me to tilt my head back.

"What if I weren't bluffing?" his voice was low, dark, delicious, and curious. "What if I'd gotten a hotel room in the city, and Fern had packed you a bag of toothbrushes and nothing else?"

My chest was airy and tight, I felt like I was floating and yet irrevocably bound to him; my words were breathless as I responded, "I guess you'd be my first kiss, and my first..."

He scrutinized me for a long moment, his eyes simmering and unsettling, but giving nothing of his thoughts away. We stood, still as statues, regarding each other as the city moved around us. It was cold and windy. A taxi's brakes screeched as it stopped at the light on Michigan Avenue. A group of friends ambled by, laughing and chatting about the show, recalling their favorite parts. Their voices ebbed and flowed and were eclipsed by new voices, new sounds.

I was contemplating whether or not I should feel silly—and had just definitively decided against it—when he lowered his eyes to my mouth, his expression still unreadable, and said, "Well then, let's go find a hotel."

***

MY BRAVADO LEFT me as soon as we crossed the threshold of the room.

If Greg hadn't asked the concierge for two toothbrushes when we'd checked in, or if the room hadn't been quite so nice, or if the bed hadn't been quite so big, I might have been able to sustain my courage for another five to ten minutes.

Alas, Greg did ask the concierge for toothbrushes. And champagne. It was on its way.

The room was nice. Extremely nice. Swanky, with a view. We were on the seventeenth floor. A window spanning carpet to ceiling overlooked downtown, the park, and Lake Michigan.

The bed was big. It was huge, and tall, with an excessive number of pillows. A single rose lay across the white duvet, slanted at an artful angle.

Everything was perfect. But it was also real. And that's why I stumbled over my feet just inside the door, the reality of my here and now catching up with me.

The door clicked shut and I flinched at the sound, holding my breath. My feelings were lodged in my throat and I couldn't have spoken a word if I tried. Greg was behind me. And he was waiting.

And waiting.

… and waiting.

I didn't move.

The distant sound of a horn blaring met my ears, followed by a blanket of heavy silence.

And still I didn't move.

So he moved.

The air shifted, growing thicker and heavier. His hands came to my shoulders, his fingers slipping into the neck of my jacket.

He bent to my neck, his lips at my ear. "Darling, let me take your jacket."

I nodded, relinquishing it, and—as a consequence—stepped further into the room. My heels were silent on the plush carpet. Beyond the walls, on the streets below, the city was muted. I wondered if the muffled hum of Chicago would be the soundtrack for… tonight.

A succinct knock on the door propelled me forward. I paced to the window and searched the darkened lawns of the park, leaving Greg to deal with the champagne and room service. People were still milling about, clusters of them, despite the lateness of the hour and the freezing temperatures and biting wind. At length, the door to our room closed again. I gathered a steadying breath and peeked over my shoulder.

Greg was standing at the high-top mini bar, untwisting the wire that held the champagne cork in place. I studied his profile and found his inscrutable mask hadn't altered. I had no idea what was going on in his head. More than the toothbrushes, the room, and the bed, his lack of expression tormented me.

Before I could ask him what he was thinking, he said, "There's something I have to tell you."

I lifted my eyebrows in expectation, glad he'd decided to both break and fill the silence. "What's that?"

Greg smoothed a hand down his tie, he'd already removed both his overcoat and his suit jacket, and spoke to the glasses he'd just poured. "As you know, I have one year left before I graduate."

He seemed to be waiting for me to reply, so I said, "Yes, I know."

"But what I haven't mentioned…" he trailed off, staring at the glasses, apparently reluctant to continue.

The hairs on the back of my neck prickled. I watched his chest rise and fall with bracing breaths. He was making me nervous.

"Greg?"

He gathered one last large inhale and finally gave me his eyes. "I'm moving to Texas."

I stood straighter, attempting to make sense of his statement. When I was certain I'd heard him correctly, I sought to clarify, "Next year, when you graduate?"

"No. I'm transferring to Texas for my senior year. I applied last fall and just received the acceptance letter last week. Their program is superior—for obvious reasons—and I have an internship lined up."

"Starting in September?" I crossed my arms.

He shook his head, pausing for a beat before admitting, "Starting in May."

"May," I echoed, my stomach falling to my feet as my eyes moved beyond him. "Oh…"

My ears were ringing.

We'd touched on the future in abstract terms—what we wanted to do with our lives, what we hoped to accomplish, graduate schools, fields of study. But we'd never spoken of definite, concrete plans involving each other. It hadn't occurred to me that the future would be so soon. It also hadn't occurred to me that we would ever be apart, now that we were together.

How silly of me. How terribly naïve.

"Fiona."

I brought my eyes back to his, silencing the ringing in my ears, and found him watching me with tense expectation.

"I leave in three weeks."

I felt dazed, like I'd been sucker punched.

I also felt like crying.

"Fe."

"Hmm?"

Greg studied me, his face persistently clear of expression. Neither of us had turned on any of the lamps in the room. The interior was illuminated exclusively by the city lights, a multifarious mixture of reds and blues, mixing to grey, and drawing long shadows on the carpet.

"Do you still want to be here, with me, tonight?"

Yes. I heard the word in my head as clearly as though it had been spoken. A resounding *yes*. Maybe even more so now, now that I knew he was leaving.

Even if Greg leaving meant he wasn't going to be my last, I still wanted him to be my first.

I wanted him to be my first everything.

I nodded, saying nothing because I didn't trust myself to speak.

His jaw ticked. He was frowning. Actually, he was scowling.

Abandoning the champagne glasses, Greg strolled to the foot of the bed, stuffing his hands in his pockets.

"Come here," he ordered.

I didn't hesitate. I moved to him, memorizing as much of the moment as possible. How his face was cast in half ashen darkness, half indirect light. His too thick hair, standing and windblown. His tie was granite grey, his shirt a crisp white, and his lips rose pink, slightly chapped. He had a freckle just under the right side of his mouth, not dark enough to be a beauty mark.

"What are you doing?"

I lifted my gaze to his, realizing I'd been staring, and answered honestly. "Remembering you."

His gaze heated, but not in the way I expected. "You realize you're too good for me, right?"

I frowned, my voice cracking as I asked, "Why would you say that?"

"Because it's true." Now his eyes moved over me like I was being memorized. "I've been so careful, taking things slow, because I wanted to fall in love with your mind and heart first, not muck it up with arms and legs and appendages. You're brilliant. And soulful. And beautiful. And clever and kind." He'd made each of the complimentary attributes sound like an insult. He looked at me like being brilliant, soulful, and the rest were character traits to be pitied.

"Well, you are all of those things, too," I countered, stepping away.

"No. Not like you." He closed the distance between us

again, gripping my sides and yanking me forward, holding me close. His next words were a rough whisper against my ear, a ragged confession, "I love you."

I love you.

Three words.

Eight letters.

Mind blown.

I lifted my hands to his chest, grabbing fistfuls of his shirt because I needed to hold on to something.

"I respect you," he continued fervently, his hot breath raising goosebumps on my skin and butterflies in my stomach. "I want to support you, I want to sacrifice for you, to forgive you, to cherish you. I want to be unconditional with you…"

I still hadn't been able to process *I love you,* therefore the rest of his speech—much like Greg himself—felt overwhelming.

"…but I don't deserve you."

I jerked my head backward to catch his eyes, not liking or appreciating his maudlin U-turn.

"I disagree." I blurted, my words emphatic, exacting.

"It's the truth." A sad smile on his lips, he pried my fingers from his shirt, gained two steps away, and let me go. He stuffed his hands back in his pockets. "Best that you know now, before things progress any further."

My temper spiked, and I opened my mouth, intent on asking what—*precisely*—that meant, because it sounded like the prelude to a breakup. I placed my fists on my hips, preparing for a fight, preparing to tell him that I loved him. Because I was pretty sure this suffocating longing and desperation to hand over my heart was, in fact, love.

I loved his goodness and wrongness, his unwavering priorities and his mulishness. I loved his patience—

granted, I also hated his patience—and I loved his wit. And I couldn't say goodbye. Not yet. And I wanted a chance to be unconditional with him, even if it was only for three weeks.

But then he knelt on the ground.

He knelt on one knee.

And he pulled a box from his pants pocket.

He looked up at me.

And I looked down at him.

He opened the box.

I covered my mouth.

There was a ring inside it.

I stared at the ring.

My vision blurred.

I stopped breathing.

The earth stopped moving.

Everything stopped.

And then he spoke, and nothing could have prepared me for the enormity of the moment.

"I'm not good enough for you, Fe. But…" he shrugged, giving me his crooked smile, "no else one is either. So I might as well take you for my own. Marry me."

The End… for now.
Fiona and Greg's story continues in 'Happily Ever Ninja'

About the Author

Penny Reid's days are spent writing federal grant proposals for biomedical research; her evenings are either spent playing dress-up and mad-scientist with her three people-children (boy-8, girl-6, girl-4 months), or knitting with her knitting group at the local coffee shop. Please feel free to drop her a line. She'd be happy to hijack your thoughts!

Come find Penny-

Mailing list signup: http://reidromance.blogspot.com/p/mailing-list-sign-up.html

Email: pennreid@gmail.com ...hey, you! Email me ;-)

Blog: http://reidromance.blogspot.com/

Twitter: https://twitter.com/ReidRomance

Ravelry: http://www.ravelry.com/people/ReidRomance (if you crochet or knit...!)

Goodreads: http://www.goodreads.com/ReidRomance

"The Facebook": http://www.facebook.com/PennyReidWriter

Please, write a review!

If you liked this book (and, more importantly perhaps, if you didn't like it) please take a moment to post a review someplace (Amazon, Goodreads, your blog, on a bathroom stall wall, in a letter to your mother, etc.). This helps society more than you know when you make your voice heard; reviews force us to move towards a true meritocracy.

Read on for:
Chapter 1 Sneak Peek of Knitting in the City #5, _Happily Ever Ninja_

Penny Reid's **Booklist** (current and planned publications)

Sneak Peek: *Happily Ever Ninja*

Happily Ever Ninja releases January 19, 2016

CHAPTER 1

Dear Husband,

I love you today more than I did yesterday. Yesterday you were a real jerk.

-Debbie
New Jersey, USA
Married 28 years

~Present Day~

Fiona

"Are we going to have sex tonight? I have stuff to do and it's already nine thirty."

"I only have fifteen minutes before I need to go pick up Grace and Jack from ballet." It may have been 9:30 p.m. for Greg, but it was only 2:30 p.m. for me. I glanced at my watch to confirm this fact. I had less than fifteen minutes. Actually, I had ten. "And we're not doing anything until you tell me why you haven't signed the transfer paperwork for the new retirement accounts."

I didn't add, *And I have a headache.* I did have a headache. I'd had a headache and no appetite for the last week, and off and on for the last month and a half, but I kept this information to myself. I didn't want to worry him.

I watched my husband sigh, his face falling into his hands. He looked tired, burnt out. He worked sixteen-hour days and usually didn't shave when he was gone. None of the rig workers did. But he must've shaved a few days ago because his chin was covered in two-day-old stubble, which only made him look more tired. But it also made him look devilishly sexy. I wished I could reach through the computer screen and give him a hug. And a kiss.

"Fine," he growled, finally lifting his head and gathering another large breath. His eyes narrowed and they darted over my form, or what he could see of it from his side of the video call. "Could you at least take off your shirt?"

"Greg."

"Show me your tits."

"Greg."

"I miss your skin, just . . . flash me."

"Greg, be serious."

"I am serious. Do I not look serious? Nothing is more serious to me than your body, specifically your tits and legs and mouth. And vagina, but the vagina goes without saying."

I gritted my teeth so I wouldn't smile, or worse, laugh. I wasn't sure how he managed it, but even when I was in a foul mood and feeling overwhelmed—like today—he always found a way to make me laugh. "Greg—"

"And your brain. Sorry, I can't believe I didn't mention your brain."

I allowed myself to give in to his sweet silliness. "I love that you mentioned my brain, because I love your brain."

With a hint of vulnerability, he asked, "But you don't love my vagina?"

I did laugh then, thankful I hadn't been sipping my coffee. Had I been drinking, it was the kind of laugh that would've sent a spray of liquid out of my mouth and nose.

The sound of his slight chuckle met my ears and was welcome; but it was also a reminder, he was trying to distract me.

I shook my head at his antics and tried to refocus. "Okay, enough about your lady closet. Mr. Jackson needs your approval to transfer the money into the new accounts. He emailed the forms three weeks ago, so why haven't you signed them yet?"

He sat back in his chair and crossed his arms, sighing for a third time. When he finally answered his voice and expression were free of all earlier playfulness. "I'm not happy with his fund choices."

I blinked at the vision of my husband, the stubborn set of his jaw. Confused, I sputtered for a full minute before spitting out an incredulous, "You approved it last month."

"But then I researched the global fund further. Over eleven percent of the principal is invested in a Monsanto subsidiary."

My headache throbbed; I nearly growled, "Then pick a different global fund."

"That's not the point. I don't like that he suggested that fund to begin with. I want to go with a different financial advisor."

My brain was going to explode all over my bedroom, which would be inconvenient since I'd just vacuumed.

I meticulously modulated my voice so I wouldn't shout my response. "Are you kidding? I've been through every investment house in Chicago and there is no one left, as according to you, everyone is either incompetent or corrupt. This has been going on for eighteen months, and meanwhile our retirement has been sitting in a low return savings account."

"Better it return nothing than we invest it in malicious corporations." He shrugged. "You know my thoughts on Monsanto."

I . . .

I just . . .

I just couldn't . . .

I took a deep breath, pushing the rage down. Greg had no way of knowing, but today was one of the worst possible days for him to deliver this news.

In addition to the unexplained headaches, I was extremely low on sleep because our daughter, Grace, had been having nightmares all week. The garbage disposal had stopped working two days ago, as had the dishwasher. Both kids had science projects due and every store in Chicago was out of poster board. Plus our son, Jack, had forgotten to give his teacher the money and slip for his field trip later in the week—he'd lost both—and I hadn't yet found five minutes to contact the woman about sorting it out.

Added to all of this, I'd just started contract work for my old engineering firm two months ago and was already behind in my latest project. Everything I touched was breaking, or broken, or a failure.

Therefore, I endeavored to be reasonable . . . or at least sound reasonable. "Pick a different fund."

His eyelids lowered and he shook his head slowly. "No. I'm not investing my money with a corrupt wanker."

"He's not a corrupt wanker. Mr. Jackson is a grandfather who volunteers his free time with the Boys and Girls Club and organizes the South Street soup kitchen. Alex checked him out—like *checked him out*—and he's completely clean." Alex was my good friend Sandra's husband, and also a world-class computer hacker. When I said Alex had checked out Mr. Jackson, I truly meant it. The man was a saint.

"Then why would he suggest a fund with an eleven percent stake in Monsanto?"

"Probably because he's trying to do his job, which is invest our money where it'll have the best return. We can pick a different fund."

He said nothing, just continued to shake his head slowly. Meanwhile I was holding on to my composure by sheer force of will. But when we ended the call I was likely going to dismember Greg's favorite boxer briefs and hide his cell phone charger. He always did this. He always found a reason not to sign.

Desperate and beyond aggravated, I scoffed, "If I show you my breasts will you sign the papers?"

Greg's eyes narrowed until he was squinting. He turned his head to the side, glaring at me as though he were both trying to discern whether or not I was being serious, and whether seeing my boobs was worth compromising his morals.

"Add an emailed photo of your ass and you have a deal."

I did growl then, and this time my face fell into my hands. If he didn't sign those transfer papers, then I would send him a picture of an ass. Maybe lots of asses. Only they wouldn't be mine. And they wouldn't be human. They would be equine.

"Fiona, darling, I'm not trying to aggravate you. You know where and how we invest is important to me." His voice was soft, beseeching, and he knew exactly what he was doing. I loved his voice; I loved his posh British accent; I loved it when he called me darling, which—after fourteen years of marriage—he rarely did anymore.

Usually I could laugh off his churlishness and bring him around to my perspective using well-reasoned arguments and my wifely wiles. But I didn't have the time or the mental energy at present to entertain my forty-one-year-old husband's plethora of opinions—opinions I usually considered endearing and charming.

For some reason, in this instance, his opinion didn't feel at all charming. It struck me as burdensome and self-indulgent. Like he was being dismissive of the work I'd done, the massive amount of time and effort I'd spent on resolving this vitally important issue.

"I have to go," I finally said, because I did have to go. But also because my head hurt and I couldn't talk to him anymore without losing my temper.

"Okay . . ."

I wasn't looking at him, my brain was full of fire ants,

but I heard the reluctance and surprise in his voice.

"Okay. Bye, Greg." I lifted my gaze and scanned the screen for the location of the courser, moving the mouse to the *end call* button.

"I love you, Fiona," he said, his voice still soft, coaxing, and maybe a little confused.

I gave him a flat smile and nodded, responding reflexively, "I love you, too."

"Don't be angry."

I shrugged. "I have to go."

"Okay, love."

"Bye."

"Wait, Fiona—"

I ended the call before he could complete his thought and immediately regretted it. I would apologize to him later. Staring at the desktop icons for a full minute, I contemplated what to do next.

I wouldn't dismember his boxer briefs. I loved it when he walked around in just his boxer briefs. He'd maintained the lithe runner's build from our college days. Even if he hadn't, I would still enjoy watching him walk around half naked, because he was my husband, he was mine and I was his. I truly adored him . . . most of the time.

But if he didn't pick a different fund and sign those papers, I was seriously considering hiding all the cell phone chargers he kept in the apartment.

I shook my head, dispelling the childish impulse, and checked my watch again. It was time to go.

As I grabbed my bag and left our apartment, a sinister

voice in my head—tired of being covered in fire ants—reminded me there was another option. I could fake his signature and never tell him, invest the money without him knowing. Just contemplating it made my stomach hurt. It was a line I wasn't ready to cross. I'd already allowed Grace—our five-year-old daughter—to have a princess costume to wear to a slumber party, and Jack—our eight-year-old son—to play soccer without Greg's consent.

I hadn't even asked Greg because I knew what he would say.

That's right. Greg had an opinion about princess costumes and boys playing sports—he was against both. I knew for a fact he hated princess culture, loathed the *Disney machinery of feminine oppression and objectification* as he called it. He'd also said in the past if Jack played sports then Grace had to as well. Which was why Jack was currently taking ballet with Grace—because if Grace took ballet, Jack had to as well. Jack didn't mind learning to dance, as long as he also got to play soccer.

But Grace didn't want to play soccer. She wanted to wear pink and play with dolls. She also loved superheroes, Legos, drawing, Darth Vader, and astronomy. She was a great kid, who happened to love dressing as a princess. So, while he was gone, I bent the rules. Just a little.

"Hey, earth to Fiona. Anyone home?"

I started, blinking as I brought my neighbor into focus. He was holding the elevator doors open, had likely said hello, and I'd been so lost to my thoughts I hadn't noticed. This level of distraction was *very* unlike me; awareness and the cataloging of my surroundings was typically second nature. Apparently, I was extremely upset.

I rushed forward into the lift and turned to give him an apologetic smile as he walked in after me. "Oh, hi. Thanks. Sorry, Matt. I'm a little preoccupied. Sorry."

He pressed the button for the lobby and stepped back to face me, tilting his head to the side, his light brown eyes assessing as they moved over my face. "Are you okay?"

"Yes. How are you?"

"Just fine," he responded slowly, openly inspecting me according to his habit.

I'd first met Matthew Simmons when I was nine. He'd been two. His parents and my parents were both unhappily married and belonged to the same country club. I babysat him a few times over the years, one of the few normal teenager activities I'd been allowed.

Matt had moved in next door to the kids and me two weeks after Christmas. I hadn't realized it was the same Matty Simmons until I'd brought him a welcome-to-the-building dinner and he'd blurted, "*Peona*!" The name he'd given me when he was a toddler.

This habit, openly scrutinizing people, was something he'd done even when he was still in diapers. And after living next door to Professor Matthew Simmons for the last two months, I knew evaluating and calculating were his adult default as well.

My smile grew more sincere the longer he scrutinized me. Matty—now Matt—had grown to be adorably peculiar and nerdy. In fact he was brazenly nerdy; but he was also nice and genuine. He'd always been nice and genuine.

Regardless, I'd had Alex run a background check on the professor—I might have been a little slap happy with the background checks, but suspicious was my default. Grace and Jack had warmed to him so quickly. The man was an open book. Undergrad at Caltech, post grad at MIT, computer scientist, associate professor at the University of Chicago, divorced two years ago and presently married to his work, terrible cook. He was also surprisingly good with kids, though he had none.

And my parents and his parents still belonged to the same country club.

"How's Grace's science fair project coming along?"

I pulled on my gloves and bobbed my head back and forth. "So-so. She convinced the kids to taste the PTC strip, but can't get them to eat the broccoli." Grace was trying to determine how many of the children in her second grade class were "super tasters", meaning more sensitive to certain foods than the rest of the population.

"Well, let me know if you need any help."

"I appreciate the offer."

"I'm not being altruistic." His dark eyebrows lifted high on his forehead, a display of pointed sincerity. "I'd do almost anything for another of your roast chicken dinners."

My grin widened. "Then why don't you come over and help Grace with her science fair project on Saturday? I was planning to make roast chicken anyway."

Matt nodded before I'd finished making the offer. "I accept," he blurted as the elevator dinged, as though marking his acceptance rather than our arrival to the lobby. We both laughed and filed out, parting ways at the entrance to the building after another few minutes of small talk.

Despite the distraction of nerdy and nice Professor Simmons, I was soon stewing in my discontent again. I stewed as I catalogued the inhabitants of the train, making note of threat likelihood, the location of exit points, and potential weapons. One man near the end of the train was holding an umbrella tucked under his arm; this was odd because it was snowing, not raining.

I kept my eyes on him when the train stopped—still stewing in my earlier frustration—and watched him as we both departed. When we exited the train station, he opened the umbrella and turned left. Apparently he didn't want any snowflakes to fall on his waterproof nylon jacket.

Delores Day's Dance Studio was on the third floor of a mixed-use brownstone, and I arrived on time. Several mothers, fathers, and nannies—all of which I recognized—were crowded around the door between the practice room and the waiting area. Kids, mostly little girls in tight buns, pink leotards, and stockings, skipped out of the classroom to their caregivers.

I nodded and smiled, chitchatted with the gathered parents about nothing in particular, and craned my neck for a glimpse of my munchkins. When they didn't appear after a few minutes, I excused myself from the circle of adults wrangling their own children and poked my head into the classroom door. Grace was sitting on the floor trying to tie her snow boots and waved at me immediately; Jack was sitting on a bench in front of a piano. His back was to me, and he appeared to be in deep conversation with their ballet teacher. Miss Delores Day was eighty at least and in better shape than most thirty year olds I knew. She was also sassier than most thirty year olds I knew.

Letting the door close behind me, I crossed the room, the sound of my footsteps drawing Delores's and Jack's attention. The older woman gave me a broad smile and glided to meet me halfway across the room with the grace of a life-long dancer.

"Mrs. Archer."

"Please, call me Fiona." I waved away the formality, my attention moving between Jack and his teacher. "Is everything all right?"

"Oh, yes. Everything is excellent. Jack was filling in for Mrs. St. Claire again. He is such a dear boy. A disinterested dancer, but a dear boy."

"Filling in?" I frowned at Delores then looked to Jack for a clue; he wasn't looking at me, his dark eyes were affixed to the keys of the instrument and I noted his cheeks were red. "Doesn't Mrs. St. Claire provide the piano accompaniment?"

"That's right. He has a real gift, though he's a bit rusty on the *Dance of the Four Swans*. More practicing at home should straighten all that out. Now, I do want to talk to you about—"

"Wait, hold on." I held my hands up to keep her from continuing. "I think one of us is confused. Jack doesn't play the piano. He doesn't play any instruments."

Delores squinted at me, as though she didn't understand my words. "What was that, dear?"

"Jack doesn't play the piano."

"Yes, he does."

"No, he doesn't."

"Well then he does a good job of pretending to play

Tchaikovsky."

"Wha-what?" Why was it suddenly hot in the dance studio?

I turned my confused frown to my son and found him watching me with a gaze too much like Greg's. His face was angelic, but his eyes held a hint of devilry and guilt.

"Jack?" I appealed to him. "What's this all about?"

He shrugged. "I've been messing around a little." I didn't miss how his fingers stroked the white keys of the piano with affection.

"Messing around?" Delores and I asked in unison.

"My dear boy, one does not mess around with Tchaikovsky's *Swan Lake*." Delores straightened her spine and sniffed in his direction, as though he'd offended her.

"When? Where?" My head was swimming and I needed to lean against something sturdy. I walked to the upright piano and placed a hand on it.

He shrugged again. "Here. At school. At Professor Simmons's."

"Have you been getting piano lessons? At school?"

"No. But Ms. Pastizo lets me in the chorus room during lunch."

"Ms. Pastizo lets you in the chorus room...?" I repeated. I was so confused. Jack was only eight, never had a music lesson, never—to my knowledge—displayed any interest in music or taking lessons. I glanced between him and the instrument. "Play something, please."

He swallowed, his gaze wide and watchful . . . and wary. "I still want to play soccer."

"What?"

"If I have to choose between music and soccer, I want to play soccer." Jack crossed his arms over his chest.

"I promised you, you can play soccer this spring and I will keep my promise." My gaze flickered to Delores, who was now watching us with dawning comprehension.

"He's never had a lesson." She made this statement to the room rather than to any one of its inhabitants, and with no small amount of wonder and awe.

Her wonder and awe made me nervous. "Jack, play Tchaikovsky. Play the Dance of the Six Ducks."

"*The Dance of the Four Swans*," Delores provided gently, coming to stand next to me.

"Yes. That one." I knew nothing about Tchaikovsky's music other than what I heard on the local NPR classical radio station. I couldn't believe my young son was capable of playing chopsticks, let alone anything so complicated.

Jack narrowed his eyes with protest, so I narrowed mine with warning. My mom-glare must've been sufficiently threatening, because he sighed loudly and placed his hands on the keys. He gave one more dramatic sigh before his eyes lost focus and he began playing.

And *ohmydearGodinheaven*, my son was playing the Jig of the Even Numbered Birds by Tchaikovsky. And he was playing it well. Remarkably well. Without sheet music. My jaw dropped and I covered my open mouth with shaking fingers.

"Oh my God."

Delores's hand closed over my shoulder and I turned my gaze to hers. She was smiling at me, a knowing smile, an elated smile. And it terrified me.

"He's never had a lesson?"

I shook my head.

"Then you know what this means."

I shook my head again—faster this time—not because I didn't know what his spontaneous piano playing meant, but because I didn't want her to say it.

"How lovely," she said, obviously not understanding the ramifications of her next words, "Jack is a prodigy."

***

"You have to take a bath."

"But the water is wet."

"That's the point of water."

"Can't I take a sand bath?"

I looked upward to the heavens beyond the ceiling of our apartment. "What are you talking about?"

"Jack says people who live in the desert take sand baths." Grace's little voice adopted an accusatory edge, as though I'd been keeping this vital piece of information from her. As thought I'd been needlessly subjecting her to the horror of wet baths for the last five years, like some sort of barbarian water-pusher.

"We don't live in the desert. We live in snowy Chicago, where water abounds—not sand."

I heard the distinct ring of my cell phone over the rush of the faucet and Grace's protests.

"But—"

"No. No more arguing, Grace. Get in the bath."

"But—"

"If I have to tell you one more time to get in the bath . . ." I turned to leave, rubbing my forehead and the sharp spike of pain radiating from my temples. If Greg were here he'd know how to get Grace into the bath without a fight. He was the master of convincing our children to brush their teeth and go to bed on time, all the while making everything fun.

Greg hardly ever being home meant it was only me, who was failing miserably at convincing my children personal hygiene was important.

Out of nowhere I was overwhelmed by a sense of longing for my husband, a need so visceral I had to stop for a second and lean against the wall, close my eyes to rein in my emotions. I wished Greg were home. I wished for him all the time.

I quickly banished the wish. He was where he needed to be. Doing good work, making a difference in the world, providing for his family. Wishing only served to make me sad. I didn't have time to be sad.

I needed to stay focused.

"I don't want a bath—"

"GRACE, GET IN THE BATH!"

"Fine," she grumbled to my back. Then I heard her pathetic wail, "I hate baths!"

And I hated yelling at my children.

I inwardly cringed as I left the bathroom and jogged to the living room. I swallowed the lump of regret in my throat as I searched for my phone. My head was full of too many thoughts, none of which brought any clarity. The fire ants had been joined by bees. The bees brought their viscous honey, slowing all processes to a virtual halt.

Shell shocked after what I'd discovered about Jack this afternoon, I'd ushered the kids out of the dance studio and gone through the motions of escorting the children home, making their dinner, assisting with homework. As usual, I argued with Grace about taking her bath and I negotiated with Jack to a half hour of playing Minecraft, and only after reading one of his chapter books for a full hour.

It was a typical evening in the Archer household: Just the three of us, me tripping over little shoes, Grace preferring dirty to clean, and Jack complaining about the distressing lack of pizza on his plate.

Except my heart was heavy with worry and my head was pounding.

I swiped my thumb across the screen of my cell phone after identifying the caller as our babysitter; my worried heart sank further. "Hi Jennifer. What's up?"

"Hi Fiona, this is Jennifer's mom. I am so sorry, but she can't babysit tomorrow night or take the kids in the morning. We just got back from the doctor's and she has strep throat."

"Oh goodness!" I dropped to the couch, rubbing my forehead with my fingers, more worry rising in my throat. I would have to find an alternate babysitter for the next night. A member of my knitting group, my good friend Ashley Winston—nurse and book worm—was moving to Tennessee.

Our close-knit band of friends had planned a going-away party for her, scheduled for tomorrow night. I'd made the cake. I'd spent all morning on it, toasting mountains of coconut for the special meringue frosting. But the real issue was Jennifer had babysat two days prior. "Well, I hope she's okay."

"The antibiotics should do the trick. You might want to keep an eye on Grace and Jack. The doctor said she might have been contagious for the last few days."

I nodded, her warning an echo to my thoughts. "I'll do that."

"Thanks. And about tomorrow morning, I am so sorry. I know this is bad timing."

It was bad timing. Jennifer was supposed to wake the kids and take them to school so I could be at the hospital by 6:00 a.m. I had an early morning MRI scheduled, part of my once-every-two-years tumor screening. I was going on sixteen years in remission, but I'd been having headaches recently, headaches I hadn't given myself permission to think about.

I had too many other things to think about.

"Don't worry about it. I hope Jennifer feels better soon."

After a few additional pleasantries, I ended the call as another of Grace's wails sailed through the apartment. "Why can't we live in the desert?"

I huffed a frustrated laugh and shook my head, collapsing back against the cushions. First things first, I needed to leave a message with the hospital about rescheduling my MRI. Then I would go through my list of alternate babysitters and try to find a replacement for Ashley's going-away party. Then I would pour myself a Julia Child-sized glass of wine—so, the entire bottle—and wrangle my adorable children who I loved (*I do, I love them, I love them . . . I do, truly*) through their bedtime routine.

Then and only then would I sort out what to do about Jack's miraculous musical acumen.

I dialed the hospital and was immediately placed on hold. While I waited, a knock on the front door pulled me from the classic rock wait music, specifically *Every Rose Has Its Thorn*. But before I could stand from the sofa, Jack bolted from his room.

"I'll get it!"

"No, you will not get it." I was hot on his heels and stopped him with a hand on his shoulder. "What are you thinking? You don't answer the door without asking first. You know that."

"But it's Professor Simmons."

"How do you know it's Professor Simmons?"

"Because he said he was going to bring me his space atlas."

"When was this?" I stepped in front of Jack and peeked through the peephole. Sure enough it was Professor Matthew Simmons.

"Yesterday. When we came home from school, remember?"

Nonplussed, I frowned as I opened the door. I didn't remember. Well, I remembered seeing Matty yesterday morning, but I didn't remember any conversation about a space atlas.

"Peona." Matt nodded his head at me in an efficient greeting, his use of the nickname inspiring a wave of nostalgia. I was pretty sure I'd never be able to look at him without seeing the toddler he used to be. Of course, since he was always wearing a vintage Star Wars T-shirt—no matter the time of day—made it difficult for me to see him as anything other than a big kid.

Matty pulled a large, hardbound book from under his arm and presented it to Jack. "Jack, the promised space atlas."

Jack grabbed it from Matty, his eyes wide and excited. "Whoa! Thanks!"

The peculiar professor grinned at my son's enthusiasm. "No problem at all."

I stepped to the side and motioned with my hand. "Won't you come in? I'm sure Jack would appreciate a tour of the atlas."

Matty didn't hesitate and quickly stepped into our apartment. "Sure, just for a bit. I don't suppose you have any leftovers from dinner?"

"Oh good Lord! You are a food addict."

"No, I'm a *good* food addict. And you make good food."

I shut the door behind him and gave him an indulgent smile. "We had spare ribs, twice-baked potatoes, and broccoli for dinner, help yourself to anything in the fridge."

"Twice-baked potatoes!? Good God, woman." His eyes bulged and he didn't need to be told twice. Matty quickly shuffled by me and sprinted for the kitchen.

Meanwhile, Jack was already on the carpet of the living room, flipping through the massive pages of the atlas. "This is so cool."

I heard the fridge open and close, the telltale sounds of jars and dishes rattling as he rummaged. "Are you sure I can have anything in here? Anything at all?" he called from the kitchen.

"Yes, help yourself." My eyes snagged on a pile of mail I must've left forgotten on the coffee yesterday. I frowned at it, feeling rising frustration at my increasing forgetfulness.

"Anything? Anything at all? Even the ca—"

"Go for it, but don't make a mess in the kitchen. Use a paper plate." I interrupted, responding absentmindedly, flipping through the mail and relieved when I found it all to be advertisements and credit card offers.

"Your kitchen is so clean, it sparkles," Matty marveled, and I heard the fridge close. "How do you do that?"

Of course, he hadn't seen the kitchen yesterday. Yesterday it was a disaster deserving of a biohazard warning. I'd spent all day yesterday and this morning picking up, cleaning, and doing laundry. It was my only chance to get the place straightened up before my Tuesday night knitting group descended. It was my week to host.

Now I just had to keep it clean for the next week . . .

"What's an alabeado?" Jack struggled to pronounce.

"Albedo," I corrected as I stood and walked to the shredding bin. "It's an attribute measurement, the reflective property of an object that isn't a source of light. Right, Matty?"

"More or less," Matty said as he shuffled back into the living room, his words garbled as he was obviously trying to talk over a mouthful of food.

I smirked as I lifted my eyes from the shredding, but then the smile fell away from my face and a cold panic hit me in the chest when I saw what he was eating.

It was cake.

It was Ashley's cake.

He was eating Ashley's cake!

Jack must've looked up and noticed the contents of Matty's plate as well, because he gasped loudly then said, "Ooooohhhh! You are in soooooo much trouble!"

The fire ants in my brain were back. My face must've communicated my despair because the look on Matty's face and his rush of words were effusively apologetic. "Oh no. I am so sorry, I'm so, so sorry! You said anything in the fridge and I love coconut and . . . oh shit, this is fucking fantastic cake."

"Ooooooooohhhh! You cussed! He cussed!" Jack stood and bounced on his feet, pointing at Matt like I might need assistance deciphering who exactly had said the expletives.

"Ahhhh!" Matty's face contorted with remorseful horror.

Jack's eyes were wide and excited. "He said fu—"

"Don't say it!" Matty and I cut him off in unison.

Jack clamped his mouth shut, looking thwarted and frustrated.

Matty groaned. "Sorry. I'm making a mess of things." Then he turned on his heel and rushed back into the kitchen. "I'll go put it back."

It took me a few seconds to move past my despairing shock, and another few to process his words—he was going to *put it back*.

"Wait, what? What are you doing?" I called as I jogged to the kitchen, "You can't put back cake. There is no putting cake back, and you've already taken a bite."

I found Matty hunched over the cake. He'd slid his wedge back into place and was using his finger to blur the line he'd made in the merengue frosting. He was making a mess.

"Stop—"

"I am so sorry, Fiona. Sometimes my stomach does the thinking and I'm powerless against it. Some people have a devil and an angel on their shoulders; I have a stomach on one side and a tongue with giant papillae on the other. And then there's my irrational love for coconut."

I grabbed his hand and removed it *and* his person from the vicinity of the cake; then I turned to assess the damage. It was beyond repair. The merengue was crushed and he'd flattened the coconut in his haste to return his piece. I sighed sadly. It looked old and tired, rumpled and ruined.

And I had an odd thought: the cake was me.

I was the cake.

I was a mess.

And I had a piece missing . . .

Peripherally I saw Jack peek into the kitchen, his big eyes moving between Matty, the cake, and me; and then he said, "It's ruined."

"Yes. Yes, it is," I said.

Jack hesitated, stepped into the kitchen, and licked his lips; hope permeated his question as he asked, "Does that mean we can eat it now?"

~End sneak peek~

Happily Ever Ninja releases January 19, 2016

Other books by Penny Reid

Knitting in the City Series
(Contemporary Romantic Comedy)
Neanderthal Seeks Human: A Smart Romance (#1)
Neanderthal Marries Human: A Smarter Romance
(#1.5)
Friends without Benefits: An Unrequited Romance
(#2)
Love Hacked: A Reluctant Romance (#3)
Beauty and the Mustache: A Philosophical Romance
(#4)
Ninja at First Sight (#4.75)
Happily Ever Ninja: A Married Romance (#5,
January 19, 2016)
Dating-*ish: A Scientific Romance* (#6 – TBD 2016)
Book #7 – TBD 2017

Winston Brother Series
(Contemporary Romantic Comedy, spinoff of *Beauty
and the Mustache*)
Truth or Beard (#1)
Grin and Beard It (#2, coming 2016)
Beard Science (#3, coming 2017)
Book #4 – TBD 2017
Book #5 – TBD 2018
Book #6 – TBD 2018

Hypothesis Series
(New Adult Romantic Comedy)
The Elements of Chemistry: ATTRACTION, HEAT,

and CAPTURE (#1)
Book #2 – TBD 2017
Book #3 – TBD 2018

Irish Players (Rugby) Series – by L.H. Cosway and Penny Reid
(Contemporary Sports Romance)
The Hooker and the Hermit (#1)
The Pixie and the Player (#2, coming March 2016)
Book #3 – TBD 2017

Made in the USA
Lexington, KY
19 June 2018